Simon Gray

SPOILED

METHUEN & CO LTD
11 NEW FETTER LANE LONDON EC4

First published in 1971
by Methuen & Co Ltd
Copyright © 1971 by Simon Gray
Printed in Great Britain
by Cox & Wyman Ltd
Fakenham, Norfolk

SBN 416 18630 0 (Hardback)
SBN 416 18630 0 (Paperback)

17 JAN 1974

for
Beryl

The first London performance of SPOILED was given at the Haymarket Theatre by Sedgemoor Productions Ltd on 24th February 1971, with the following cast in order of appearance:

HOWARTH	Jeremy Kemp
DONALD	Simon Ward
JOANNA	Anna Massey
LES	Peter Denyer
MRS CLENHAM	Pamela Pitchford

The play was designed by Anthony Holland, lit by Joe Davis and directed by Stephen Hollis.

ACT ONE

Scene One

The stage is divided. Three-quarters of the stage space, on the right, shows the living-room and one quarter, on the left, shows a small spare room, referred to in the directions that follow as the bedroom. A wall with a door upstage, opening into the bedroom, divides the two rooms.

The living-room is large, comfortable, middle-class intellectual and casual. A table with books and a lamp stands in the window and against the wall downstage of the window a smaller table also with books and a lamp. Against the wall upstage of the window is an old upright piano and piano stool. The main door to the rest of the house is facing us upstage right. Through this door can be seen the hall, with the foot of stairs upstage. The kitchen can be seen through a hatch, which is on the left of the main door in the living-room. Running along the back wall of the living-room, under the hatch, is a shelf-unit with a lamp, a tray of drinks and a hi-fi unit on it. The speakers for the hi-fi are on a shelf above. Books fill other shelves on the back wall and shelves above the piano.

The bedroom area, left, has baby paper on the walls and is cluttered with a desk against the back wall, with a lamp and two single chairs, a carry-cot against the dividing wall downstage and parts of a larger cot upstage of the door. A folding bed, made up and hidden with a cloth cover is folded and stands against the wall, left.

The action starts in the living-room.

HOWARTH *and* DONALD *are seated at the table,* HOWARTH *in the elbow chair right,* DONALD *left.* DONALD *has a bicycle satchel on the floor beside him,* HOWARTH *has text books on the table in front of him and a brief case on the floor. As the curtain rises* DONALD *stoops to pick up three text books which he has knocked on to the floor.* HOWARTH *is eating a biscuit.*

HOWARTH. In the event of almost any catastrophe "je suis desolé" will do nicely.

DONALD. Um, je suis desolé.

HOWARTH. Yeah. A phrase like that's worth five marks in the oral. It might be worth contriving a small accident, like stumbling over the examiner's toes, to get it in. Don't hurt him, mind.

DONALD *laughs.*

O.K. Expliquez-moi, monsieur Donald Clenham, pourquoi vous êtes en train d'apprendre le français?

DONALD (*nervously*). Um, um, parce-que je veux apprendre le français.

HOWARTH (*waits, smiles*). Elaborate. Don't be afraid of boring him.

DONALD. Um, um, parce-que je veux voyager en France et parce que il est, um, c'est une langue très intéressant.

HOWARTH. Now Donald, think. (*Pause.*) Une langue intéressant?

DONALD. Oh, um. (*Laughs.*) Um, un langue intéressant. Um ....

HOWARTH (*looks at him, eyebrows raised*). Well, at least now you're consistent. But wrong.

DONALD (*after a ghastly pause*). Une langue intéressante ... (*Tentatively.*)

HOWARTH. Mmm, huh. O.K. (*Smiles.*) Can you relax? You're terribly tense today. Why?

DONALD. No, I'm all right. Well ...

HOWARTH. Is it because the exam's on Monday?

DONALD (*shakes his head*). Well ... I suppose I keep thinking about it, sir.

HOWARTH. Don't make it worse than it is. Look, today's Saturday. You've got all day tomorrow. Don't suffer before you have to. What are you going to do for the rest of the weekend?

DONALD (*shrugs*). Nothing really. Go for a bicycle ride with a friend and ... well, do some work.

HOWARTH. Fine. But don't do too much, eh? Get your mother to throw you out of the house, to the cinema or something, eh?

DONALD *nods*.

No, really. I'm all for your translating a few passages, but for God's sakes don't work yourself into a state. In fact, I'll give you a ration of passages to take home, and you stick to those. (*Rises, goes up to hatch, brings out a biscuit tin, helps himself to a biscuit.*) Mm? (*Looks at him, smiles.*) By the way, there's something I've been meaning to ask you. What have you been using for a dictionary?

DONALD. Just a um, little one.

HOWARTH. Got it with you?

DONALD *nods. Then, clearly embarrassed, he bends over, picks up his satchel, fumbles in it and picks an exercise book out of the satchel. A folded picture from a magazine drops from the exercise book on to the floor.*

DONALD. The thing is, my mum got it for me. (*Picks a very small dictionary out of the satchel, holds it up.*) She just went into the shop and asked for one and this is the one they, um ...

HOWARTH. Keep it for a weekend in Paris. (*Hands him the little one and picks up an enormous Cassells dictionary from the table.*) But you borrow this one for this weekend, eh? (*Hands him the big one.* DONALD *notices the photograph on the floor and hurriedly puts his foot over it.* HOWARTH *sees this.*) It's an extremely lucky dictionary. Even if you don't use it, it'll communicate a certain impressive confidence. I've lent it to hundreds of boys at school just before exams, and always with satisfactory results. Let it calm you down.

DONALD. Thank you, sir. I'll bring it back afterwards, straight away.

HOWARTH. O.K. Are you up to a dictation?

> DONALD *grabs the photo from the floor and puts it in his satchel.* HOWARTH *notices this.* DONALD *nods, draws an exercise book to him.*

Let's see. (*Flicking through the pages of a text-book.*) What with you twice a week and five classes at school twice a week, I can never remember. (DONALD *puts the dictionary in his satchel and looks through his exercise book.*) 'Ce matin-là Jean avait parlé beaucoup des blés et de ce qu'il appelait la "culture intensive" . . .?

DONALD. Yes, we've done that one, sir.

Un homme voyageait dans un pays de montagnes . . . (HOWARTH *looks at* DONALD, DONALD *nods.*) Yeah, I remember that, um, 'Il y a, à Vérone, des jardins'.

> DONALD *shakes his head.*

HOWARTH. All right. (*Gets up, saunters to the window, puts his hand in his pocket.*) Ready?

> DONALD *nods, pushes his satchel clumsily aside.*

'Il y a, à Vérone, des jardins à l'italienne où l'on monte par une série d'escaliers et de terrasses. J'y passai l'après-midi dans un terrible perplexité. D'en haut, je découvrais . . .'

> DONALD, *as* HOWARTH *reads, is still clumsily attempting to get ready . . . He knocks the satchel off the table, kneels, shoves papers and books back inside.*

DONALD (*gets up, is desperately scrabbling*). Sorry, sir.

> HOWARTH *stands watching, as* DONALD *sits down, and gets a pencil out of his pencil case.*

Um, sorry sir.

HOWARTH. All right? 'Il y a, à Vérone.' (HOWARTH *continues to read the dictation piece.* DONALD *breaks the point of his pencil, scrabbles in the pencil case for a sharpener and starts to sharpen his pencil over the satchel.* HOWARTH *notices this and breaks off.*) This isn't a good idea. Not now, anyway. Shall we give it a rest?

DONALD (*sits looking down at the table, mutters inaudibly*). Sorry, sir.

HOWARTH. Mmmmm. (*Looks at him thoughtfully.*) Donald, if the worst comes to the very worst, and you don't *feel* like it on Monday morning, you can always take it the next time around, can't you?

DONALD *nods.*

So why does it matter so much? You know, I'm generally telling boys at this stage that they've got to care more. In your case perhaps you should really try caring less.

DONALD (*nods again*). Except, well. (*Looks at him.*) It's my mum, sir. She's expecting me to get it, and – because it's the third time and that. (*Laughs.*)

HOWARTH. She'll be angry with you?

DONALD. No, no, she won't – no, but she, well . . . worries.

HOWARTH. Parents do tend to. Especially mothers.

DONALD. Yes, sir.

HOWARTH (*pause, looks at him, as if thinking*). Look, do you think she'd spare you for the weekend?

DONALD. Sir?

HOWARTH. Then we could take things at their own pace, eh? We could get through a bit of work, and calm each other down. I'd hate to think that all we've done over the last six weeks is going to slip away in a nervous weekend. (*Pause.*) Eh?

DONALD. Well . . . (*Stops, stares at him blankly.*)

HOWARTH. Do you think she'd mind?

DONALD *shakes his head.*

Or would *you* rather not?

DONALD (*looks down, mutters shyly*). Don't want to put you out, sir.

HOWARTH. I wouldn't have asked you if I thought you'd be putting us out. We'd both be delighted to have you. So the question for you to answer, frankly and fearlessly, is whether you want to. Do you?

DONALD (*nods, looking down*). Thank you very much indeed, sir.

HOWARTH. Good. Very good. Now we *can* relax ... although, first you'd better phone your mother.

DONALD. Sir. (*Gets up.*)

HOWARTH. It's just in the hall there.

DONALD. Sir. (*Nods, walks across the room.*)

> HOWARTH *stands for a moment, stroking his chin, then makes a sudden face, as if grasping that he's done something he hadn't really intended. He spots* DONALD's *satchel, looks down at it, starts to bend to pick it up.*

(*Reappears at the door.*) Um, the only thing, um, we're not on the telephone.

HOWARTH. Oh. Well, you'll have to let her know, of course. Is there anyone else you could phone? You could ask *them* to ask *her* to phone us or ... (*Shrugs.*) It's very complicated, isn't it?

DONALD. Well, there's some people next door – sometimes they let us use their phone.

HOWARTH. There you are then.

DONALD. Sir. (*Goes out.*)

> HOWARTH *shakes his head, bends down and takes out the folded paper, opens it, looks at it, makes a little whistle of amused surprise ... is about to put it back into the satchel, when the door opens and* DONALD *reappears. He shoves the folded paper into his back pocket.*

I just remembered, um. (*Laughs awkwardly.*) They're away this weekend. They've gone to visit her auntie ... she lives in Bexhill.

HOWARTH. Oh dear. Well, perhaps we'd better think again. I

can't keep you here without letting your mother know, and it's
scarcely worth your cycling all the way home and back again.

DONALD. I don't mind, sir. I mean, it wouldn't take me long.

HOWARTH. Your mother might not be in.

DONALD. Oh, yes sir. She doesn't go out until later. She's doing
the matinée . . . that's at two-thirty.

HOWARTH (*reluctantly*). Well, in that case . . .

The sound of the door slamming.

JOANNA (*off*). Hello!

JOANNA *opens the door. She is carrying a bundle of clothing . . .
scarlet, curtain-like, and a plastic carrier-bag.*

HOWARTH. Though it seems rather a business . . .

JOANNA (*entering between them, looks at* DONALD). Hello, Donald
– it is Donald, isn't it?

HOWARTH (*as* DONALD *smiles, nods awkwardly*). Yes. Donald
Clenham.

JOANNA (*shaking hands with* DONALD). Well, hello, Donald.

DONALD. Um, hello, um . . .

JOANNA. I've got your gear. (*Drops the stuff on the couch.*) I've
just got to nip up to the butcher for the joint. I won't be long.

HOWARTH. O.K.

JOANNA *smiles, goes to the kitchen door and through.*

Well, what do you think? (*To* DONALD.) If it *is* going to be
difficult. Mmmm?

JOANNA (*reappearing from the kitchen*). Have you finished, or are
you going on a bit?

HOWARTH. Actually, we were just deciding that very question.
Why?

JOANNA. Well, I just thought if you *were* going on, why doesn't
Donald stay and have a bite . . . only scrambled eggs on Saturday, I'm afraid. (*To* DONALD.)

DONALD. Mmm, well . . . mmm . . . (*Laughs, looks at* HOWARTH.)

HOWARTH. As a matter of fact, darling. (*Laughs.*) The question we were attempting to decide was whether or not Donald should stay for the weekend.

JOANNA (*looks at him, a fractional pause*). Oh, lovely. (*To* DONALD.) Do.

HOWARTH. That is, if we're all right for sheets and things.

JOANNA. We are. (*Smiling over-politely directly at* HOWARTH.)

HOWARTH. Actually, there are *other* problems. We can't think how to get hold of Donald's mother.

JOANNA. Donald's mother? (*After a pause.*) She'd be very welcome too, of course.

HOWARTH (*laughs again*). No no . . . to let her know where Donald is.

JOANNA (*laughs*). Oh, I see. (*Suddenly naturally.*) Oh, manage it somehow please, Donald. We'd love you to.

HOWARTH (*in relief*). Yes, come on now, Donald, let's think.

JOANNA (*looks at* HOWARTH). Well, I'll see you later. (*Looks at* DONALD.) Both of you, I hope.

Severe look at HOWARTH *as she goes out, shutting the door.*

HOWARTH (*smiles*). There you are, you see. My old lady isn't a problem, I'm sure yours won't be.

DONALD. No. Well, I'll go around on my bike then.

HOWARTH. Good. That *is* settled then, isn't it? At last. (*Pause.*) Do you want to go now, or shall we have another go at that dictation?

DONALD (*pause*). I don't mind. I mean, well, the dictation . . . if that's all right.

HOWARTH *goes to the box and picks it up.* DONALD *sits down at the table.*

HOWARTH. 'Ce matin-là Jean avait parlé beaucoup de blès et de ce qu'il appelait la "culture" . . .' No, that wasn't the one. Ah, 'Il y a, à Vérone, des jardins à l'italienne . . .' (*Stops.*) Have you ever thought that the major stresses in life come from the most minor embarrassments? Mmm – I mean, that we spend an enormous amount of energy and feeling on the most trivial worries . . . the ones that we forget about almost immediately. Mmmm?

DONALD *smiles, bewildered.*

A random thought, and not worth interrupting a dictation for . . . Now – 'Il y a, à Vérone des jardins a l'italienne où l'on monte par une série d'escaliers et de terrasses. J'y passai l'après-midi dans une terrible perplexité. D'en haut, je . . .'

DONALD, *during this, has secretly looked anxiously at his watch. He holds up his hand for attention, like a child in class, looking towards* HOWARTH *in a panic.*
HOWARTH *stops and looks at him.*

DONALD. She leaves for the cinema at two, for the matinée.
HOWARTH. Yeah?
DONALD. Well, if I go later, I may be too late.
HOWARTH. Oh. Well then, you'd better go now, hadn't you? (*Snaps the book shut, smiles.*) Get it over with once and for all, anyway. This could go on all afternoon.

There is a ring at the bell.

Is that all settled, then? (*Smiling, goes out of the room.*)

DONALD *puts on his jacket and looks hurriedly through his satchel.*

HOWARTH (*off, at the front door*). Yes?
LES (*off*). Sorry to interrupt. My name's Les. I'm looking for Donald Clenham.
HOWARTH (*off*). Oh, come in, come in.

The door opens. HOWARTH *comes back in, accompanied by* LES.

HOWARTH. For you, Donald. Les. (*Looking at* LES.)

DONALD *puts down the satchel.*

LES. Hello, Don. I'm sorry to interrupt. You said half-past and I thought perhaps I'd missed you ... that you'd already gone. There was another turning you could have meant. I thought I'd been waiting at the wrong one.

DONALD. I'm sorry. I – I ... (*Looks at* HOWARTH, *then at* LES *again*.) ... forgot.

LES. That's all right. (*Pause*.) Do you want me to wait on a bit, then? Or what?

DONALD. Well, I can't come, you see.

LES. Oh. (*Little pause*.) That's all right.

HOWARTH (*who has been looking at* LES). I'm sorry, the fault is entirely ours. We persuaded Donald to stay for a bit, and in the confusion of arrangements *everything* got forgotten.

LES. That's all right. It doesn't matter. We were only going for a ride. (*Pause*.) It doesn't matter.

HOWARTH (*to* LES). I know you, don't I?

LES. I was at St Martin's for a while, sir.

HOWARTH. Yes, I thought you were. About three years ago.

> LES *nods*.

Grant. Leslie Grant.

LES (*nods*). I never had you for French, I was in Mr Wales's class. I was only there for two years ... and Mr Holliday's.

HOWARTH. You left early, didn't you?

LES. Sir. (*Slightly embarrassed*.)

HOWARTH (*pause*). What are you doing now?

LES. Same as Don ... I'm in Crabtree's.

HOWARTH. Oh. Which part?

LES (*laughs, embarrassed again*). Well, in cutlery ... at the moment. Mainly I'm on sales in cutlery, sometimes in toys.

HOWARTH. And do you like that?

LES. Well, not too much. (*Looks towards* DONALD.) Eh, Don?

> DONALD *laughs awkwardly. Pause.*

HOWARTH. I'm sorry. Still, you'll probably be able to move on ... or out.

LES. We hope so. (*To* DONALD *again*.) Eh, Don?

DONALD *again laughs awkwardly.*

HOWARTH. Well, I'm sorry I've mucked up your Saturday ride.

LES. No, it doesn't matter. We can go tomorrow, can't we, Don?

A slight pause.

DONALD. Well, I'll be here tomorrow, Les, actually.

LES (*pause, still quite easy*). Oh. (*Pause.*) Oh well, that's that, then. It doesn't matter.

HOWARTH. But look here, if you're going to be in this area – I mean, if you feel like coming out – do drop in for a cup of coffee or tea.

LES. Oh no, I wouldn't want to interrupt . . .

HOWARTH (*pause*). You wouldn't be. We're bound to need a break. The idea is to get a bit of French into Donald in as relaxed a way as possible.

LES. Oh, well, that's very kind of you. Thanks very much. I don't know if I will be in the area . . .

HOWARTH. No, but if you are.

LES. Well, thank you, sir.

HOWARTH. How extraordinary, you two knowing each other. You never told me you knew an old St Martin's boy, Donald.

DONALD. Well, Les said . . .

LES. I said I was sure you wouldn't remember me.

HOWARTH. You see, I do. I was sorry you . . . had to leave.

LES. Yes. (*Little pause.*) So was I. I might have learnt some French. (*Laughs.*)

HOWARTH (*laughs*). Well, um, Donald, if you're going to see your mother . . . we've been trying to think of ways of letting Donald's mother know that he's staying with us.

LES. Oh, I'll tell her. I might as well go back anyway.

HOWARTH *looks at* DONALD.

DONALD. Oh, well, thanks, Les. Thanks.

LES. No trouble. It's only just around the corner from us.

(*To* HOWARTH.) If she's not there, I'll put a note through the letter box, O.K.?

HOWARTH. Perhaps you'd better give her our phone number . . . 6371.

LES. 6371. I always remember numbers. (*Smiles at* DONALD.) Good luck for Monday if I don't see you, Don.

DONALD. Thanks.

LES. Goodbye, then.

HOWARTH. Goodbye.

> LES *goes out.*

Perhaps under the circumstances, you should see Les down the path, eh?

> DONALD *nods, and hurries out.*
>
> HOWARTH *stands for a moment, then moves up to the hatch, reaches through for the biscuit tin and takes a biscuit. There is the sound of the front door. He crams the biscuit into his mouth, gulps it down hurriedly.* JOANNA *comes in with the shopping bag, stands looking at him ironically.*

(*Swallows furtively.*) I know. Don't say it.

JOANNA. But has he mysteriously doubled? I passed two of him cycling down the path.

HOWARTH (*laughs*). No, just a friend he'd arranged to meet.

JOANNA. Ah, gone to get more friends for the weekend perhaps? Will they come back as four? (*Goes out into the kitchen.*)

HOWARTH. Darling, I'm terribly sorry. But I did apologise.

JOANNA (*returning*). Did you? How?

HOWARTH. I kept glancing at you abjectly.

JOANNA. Well, what came over you?

HOWARTH. I don't know.

JOANNA. Richard, I ask compassionately.

HOWARTH (*pause, shakes his head, takes her hand and speaks directly to her, kindly*). Well, I do know. He's got his 'O' level or Monday – he's failed twice already – and he's in a state about it. He lives alone with a repressively anxious and Catholic mother, who'll almost certainly demoralise him thoroughly before the weekend's out. So, I thought . . . (*Shrugs.*) It might just make the difference. (*Pause, kisses her hand.*) *Do* you mind?

JOANNA. Yes. (*Hand on his shoulder.*) But I'd be a bitch if I made a fuss, wouldn't I? When the cause is so good. (*Kisses him.*)

HOWARTH. Well, how are you, then?

JOANNA. Roughly as you see me. I've had a very stimulating morning. I asked Matthews why there was a layer of beef around the fat, like a blanket to keep it warm, and at the supermarket I caused – and then took part in – a scene about the size and colour of the eggs. I wanted large brown ones and they had tiny white ones, that look as if the chickens have stamped them out with machines. In other words, I succeeded in making myself into a harridan, and in the fridge I've got beefy fat, and a dozen shiny, white little eggs.

HOWARTH. Poor darling.

JOANNA. Yes. How did you get landed with him in the first place?

HOWARTH. Who? Donald? He's the one that Catholic priest wrote to the school about – O'Toole, Father O'Toole. His dad died when he was three, his mother's had to work to keep them both. He didn't do too well at school, is now doing something or other at that shop you hate – Crabtree's – and wants to better himself, I suppose. After his French he's going to try for maths and a few other subjects – with Father O'Toole's letters to help, no doubt . . . if he gets his French.

JOANNA. And will he?

HOWARTH. It depends, I should say, almost entirely on his nerve, and whether he knows enough. No, probably not. His nerve is bad and he doesn't know enough.

JOANNA. But you're going to have a go?

HOWARTH. Yes.

JOANNA. All right. But you shall make it up to me. What with vanishing for rehearsals while I sew up your costumes, introducing nervous boys into the house, and no doubt a brief-case full of marking . . .

HOWARTH. I shall – make it up to you.

JOANNA. But there's something else. (*Sternly.*) You've been at the biscuits.

HOWARTH. What?

JOANNA. What? (*Imitating him.*) The crumbs are clustered around your lips. (*Pokes him in the stomach.*) You're . . . (*Poke.*) . . . not . . . (*Poke.*) . . . to . . . (*Poke.*) It's bad for you to be fat. (*Slaps him.*) And it's self-indulgence, and on top of which . . .

The door opens, DONALD *comes in, stops and looks at them awkwardly.*

(*As* HOWARTH *steps away.*) Oh, hello. How did you get in?

DONALD (*pause*). The door was on the latch.

JOANNA. Of course it was. (*Laughs.*) Well, you've fixed it all up, which is lovely.

HOWARTH. We really must do that dictation. Come on, Donald, we'll go next door until lunch.

JOANNA. It's very cluttered in there.

HOWARTH. It's all right. Besides, we'll be out of your way.

JOANNA (*as* HOWARTH *and* DONALD *go out*). But you don't have to be.

HOWARTH *appears not to have heard.*
Blackout.

Scene Two

That Evening.

In the small room, DONALD *kneels searching in his satchel, takes out a copy of 'Mayfair' and shakes it, puts it back, goes quietly to dividing door and opens it very carefully. He sees there is no-one about, so enters and looks on table, sits left of table and starts silently to rehearse the moment when he dropped the photograph, putting his foot out in the way he did before. Still puzzled, he kneels left of the table to look under it. As he does so* JOANNA *enters.*

DONALD *starts, rises.*

JOANNA (*closing door*). Did I frighten you?

DONALD. Um, pardon, I didn't know. I was looking for Mr Howarth ... I mean, whether he was back yet.

> JOANNA, *behind the sofa, takes one of the cushions from the left end to the right end, preparatory to sitting there.*

JOANNA. No, he's still rehearsing – at least I presume he is. These school plays are meant to be for the students, but every year he always seems to grab a small, but plum, part for himself. This time he's one of those bishops in Henry Fifth, which means a lovely costume for him and hours of needlework for me. Were you looking for him under the table?

DONALD (*laughs falsely*). No, there was a bit of paper, um, it must have fallen out of my satchel.

JOANNA (*looks around the floor*). In here?

DONALD. No, it's probably in there. It wasn't anything important. (*Little pause, then goes back into room.*)

JOANNA. Where are you going?

DONALD. Well, I'd better get back ...

JOANNA. Oh, do sit down. You can't spend the whole time here working, and besides, we've scarcely exchanged a word all day.

DONALD. Well, I haven't finished that translation passage he set me.

JOANNA (*smiles*). Sit down, please. (*With quiet authority.*)

DONALD *looks at her, comes across, sits down.*

(*Picks up the edge of the material, and the needle, begins to sew – suddenly laughs.*) Very satisfactory. I'm trying out a completely new technique – quiet authority – and it works ... at least, it does with you. You can go now if you insist.

DONALD. No, that's all right.

JOANNA. Are you very on edge? Before an examination is hell, isn't it?

DONALD. No, I don't feel too bad this time. Not really.

JOANNA. Good for you. (*Smiles, pauses.*) You work at that big shop – Crabtree's.

DONALD. Yes.

JOANNA. It's very grand. I only go there on days when I feel impregnable. Which I'm certainly not at the moment. What do you do exactly?

DONALD. Well, I help out in accounts.

JOANNA. Oh, *do* you? You must have a very good head for figures, then?

DONALD. No, I just, you know, take the letters around and – that.

JOANNA. I see. Anyway, you're not one of the supercilious salesmen – the ones who put people like me in their places?

DONALD. Um, no. No. (*Laughs.*)

There is a silence.

JOANNA. I did have one very nice experience in Crabtree's. When I was working on the *Argus* – which, come to think of it, was up to three months ago – being pregnant makes me feel that anything before that was about six years away. (*Laughs,* DONALD *smiles dimly.*) Well, it was my first year as a reporter, a real reporter, and I remember I went in to buy something very ordinary – spoons, I think – and they only had these Swedish things at about nine and six each, and the boy said why didn't I try Woolworth's. So, I made one of my scenes, and it ended up with my seeing the manager, who was very snooty ... (DONALD *laughs*.) ... and said much the same thing – I really could have murdered him. Well, the next week I got my first real assignment, which was to interview the manager of Crabtree's about a special fair or sale they were having. It was delicious, strutting impassively into his office.

DONALD *laughs again, evidently realising it's expected.*

Unfortunately, I was far too green and nervous to take advantage. *Now* I would have murdered him this side of libel. (*There is a long, appalling silence.*) I don't know what on earth he's up to. He was meant to be back ... (*Looks at her watch.*) ... half an hour ago. I expect he's got involved – some lame duck – (*Embarrassed.*) I mean, some wretch who can't get his lines right – um, tell me. (*Hurriedly.*) What's he like as a teacher? I always hear from him what his pupils are like, but never from them what he's like.

DONALD (*looks at her, looks down*). Well, he's very good. (*In a mumble.*)

JOANNA. I don't mean he's ever gossiped about you – except in the most flattering way. (*Laughs.*) God, how awful. It must sound as if I'm fishing, but I can't help taking advantage. You know, you're the first of his pupils I've ever had a chance to grill. (*Waits.*)

DONALD. Well, he's got a very good accent.

JOANNA (*laughs*). Yes, that must be quite a help.

DONALD (*pause*). And, um, well, it's when he explains something, then I understand it. When my teachers at school used to explain things, I didn't always understand ... not really.

JOANNA. Ah, I see. He makes you want to learn, is that it?

DONALD. Well, if I go on getting it wrong, then it's like I'm sort of – well, you know, letting him – Mr Howarth – down.

JOANNA. There you are, you see. I've been married to a teacher for three years. My teachers ... I either hated them and ragged them unmercifully, or I had the most ghastly crushes on them. (*Laughs.*)

DONALD, *puzzled, laughs.*

Which is why I'm probably so uneducated.

DONALD (*nervous laugh*). Yes ...

JOANNA. Oh dear, (*Yawns.*) I feel sleepy all the time these days. It's because I eat so much. I hope you haven't been letting him pilfer cakes and biscuits from the kitchen. He's on a diet this term – next term he's doing the football, so I can let him relax a little.

DONALD *nods.*

Does he? Steal from there? (*Gestures towards the kitchen.*)

DONALD. Steal? No, no. Well, I don't know.

JOANNA. Mm. He's very sly. I find chocolate and biscuit crumbs in his pockets. (*Pause.*) Well, I could find worse, I suppose. (DONALD *gives a little giggle* – JOANNA *looks at him* – *she yawns again.*) Oh dear, I'm sorry. I suppose I might as well go to bed, if I'm going to. (*Stretches.*)

DONALD *gets up.*

No, why don't you stay here. It's much more comfortable.

DONALD. Well, I've got my stuff in there, um ...

JOANNA. Oh. Well, in that case, *I'll* stay on the sofa. (*Swings her legs up.*) There!

DONALD (*uncertainly*). Well. (*Sits down.*) Um ...

JOANNA. You *can* go, if you want. I shan't take offence.

DONALD. No, it's all right.

JOANNA. Well. (*Smiles.*) It's very nice of you. (*Pause.*) You will excuse me if I just close my eyes ... and you pop off the second you want to. (*Closes her eyes, keeps them closed.*)

DONALD, *after a moment, looks at her, kneels and looks under the table again.*

The sound of a door closing downstairs.
DONALD *retreats back into his bedroom with the satchel. He sits at his desk and writes out a translation during the following scene.* JOANNA *sits up.*
HOWARTH *comes in, with his brief-case.*

JOANNA. Well? (*Looks at her watch.*)

HOWARTH. I'm sorry. There was a bad case of stage fright. I had to do some soothing down. How are you, then?

JOANNA. Intolerant.

HOWARTH. Oh. Not of me, I hope.

JOANNA. Only by association.

HOWARTH. Oh. Where is he?

JOANNA. Oh – smoking pot in the kitchen, or out in the fields raping a peasant . . . Or, yes, possibly next door in one of his more serious moods having a go at his French, do you think?

HOWARTH. Well, I'd better go in.

JOANNA. No, you don't. (*Takes him by the wrist.*) He's only just gone – you can spare me five minutes. *He* did.

HOWARTH. Oh? What did you talk about?

JOANNA (*pulls him down beside her, puts her arms around him*). Well, he wanted to know about our sex life. (*Taking his arm.*) Very prying, and slightly coarse in his approach. Lost his temper and called me a swollen tart – said he was looking forward to the day when you and me and our kind were swept aside. Frankly, some of his ideas struck me as a little wild, but he'll probably settle down in a few years' time and have babies like the sad rest of us.

HOWARTH. You don't like him, then?

JOANNA. How would I know? He's been here all day, in a trance of shyness at lunch and supper, and concealed from view for the rest of the time. But I do just wonder why, of all the pupils you've ever taught, this is the only one I get a chance to look at.

HOWARTH. He's a special case. None of the boys at school need this sort of attention – for obvious reasons.

JOANNA. Really, I'm not against him, you know. It just seems odd, in this day and age. It's not as if I was being *de haut en bas* to him. He was being *de bas en haut*, or whatever it is, to me.

HOWARTH. He wasn't. It doesn't exist.

JOANNA. Don't school-teach me, thank you.

HOWARTH. Sorry.

JOANNA. You are prickly, aren't you? All through lunch you behaved as if I were going to assault him – warning glances at me, protective smiles for him.

HOWARTH. Well, it was an ordeal for him.

JOANNA. Thank you. (*Laughs.*) Oddly enough, he makes *me* feel quite shy – which is why I chattered at him. Does he have any girl friends?

HOWARTH. I don't know. He's just as inaccessible to me, darling. (*Mitigatingly.*)

JOANNA. Well, you're not inaccessible to him. He managed a few words about you.

HOWARTH. Oh? (*Little pause.*) What?

JOANNA. He said he liked to please you. That's why you're a good teacher. (*Pause.*) No, that's what it came to. What he really meant, of course, was that you've got a sexy personality. (*Little pause.*) And you're very self-indulgent.

HOWARTH. Self-indulgent? It's . . . (*Looks at his watch.*) . . . ten-thirty on a Saturday evening. I've been cramming Donald all day, and ever since supper I've been rehearsing a school play – and shortly I shall have to mark exercises for Monday – after, that is, a spell with Donald again.

JOANNA. You're not!

HOWARTH. I've got to.

JOANNA. Can't you do them tomorrow?

HOWARTH. Yes, but I shall have to do a few of them tonight as well. Donald's not the only one taking his 'O' levels next week.

JOANNA. Well, bloody hell, it sounds like self-indulgence to me.

It's only because it's a respectable activity that you get away with it. You know, I could, if I were feeling nasty, remind you that last weekend, which you spent almost entirely at rehearsals, you only managed to calm me by promising me this weekend – all to myself.

HOWARTH (*stacking exercise books in a pile on the table*). I know. I have apologised.

There is a silence.

JOANNA. Doesn't he have any friends at all?

HOWARTH. Friends? Who? Donald? (*Looks through O-level dictation book.*) I don't know. He's got one – the one that came this morning. I suppose he's got friends, like any other ordinary young man.

JOANNA. Not so ordinary. He's too pretty to be ordinary. Even if he's totally innocent about his looks now – of course, when he finds out, he'll probably turn into a monster.

HOWARTH. Then I shall have to watch him with you, won't I?

JOANNA. Oh, don't worry. I'd never have fancied him.

HOWARTH. Poor Donald. Why not? (*Starts to correct an exercise book.*)

JOANNA. Perhaps because he'd never have fancied me. He seems to get on best with the older man. (*Giggles.*) Anyway, this is a bit strong – I'm meant to be the one in the interesting condition and we spend all our time talking about how ... (DONALD *opens the door, coughs awkwardly.*) ... uninteresting your house guest is.

DONALD. Um, I'm – I've finished that, sir.

HOWARTH. Poor Donald – I didn't mean to keep you, uh ... (*Gets up.*) Anyway, I'll join you now.

JOANNA. Donald can join *you* – in here. It's much more comfortable, and I'm going to bed. And, by the way Donald, I've made him confess – he eats cakes and biscuits with you, doesn't he?

DONALD, *as* HOWARTH *smiles irritably, stares at her, then at him.*

You might as well come clean too.

DONALD. Oh no, he doesn't eat anything.

JOANNA. You've never even seen him eat *one* biscuit?

DONALD. No. No, I haven't.

JOANNA (*looks at him, slightly startled*). You know, I don't believe you, though thousands would. (*Laughs.*)

DONALD *laughs and looks at* HOWARTH, *who raises a stiff smile.*

JOANNA. Anyway, you're to be my ally tomorrow. You're to leave fatter than when you came, and he's to be . . . (*Punching* HOWARTH's *stomach.*) . . . thinner when you leave.

HOWARTH. It sounds like a very good way to reduce me. (*Sharply to* JOANNA.) You'd better go and get your books then, Donald.

DONALD *goes out, leaving his door open.*
HOWARTH *turns away, walks to the table, and sits.*

JOANNA (*sotto voce*). You're not prickling again. I was only trying to cover up.

HOWARTH. It's all right.

JOANNA. Do you think he heard?

HOWARTH. I hope not.

JOANNA. You're not very reassuring.

HOWARTH. Well, I can't *be* sure, can I?

The door opens again. DONALD *comes in, carrying his satchel. He comes to the table.* JOANNA *sits on the sofa and starts to sew.*

JOANNA. By the way, Donald, did you find your bit of paper?

DONALD. Um, no.

JOANNA. I'll keep my eye open for it.

DONALD. No, it doesn't matter, it's nothing. Just a stupid – picture. *I* don't want it. (*Violently.*)

JOANNA. I see.

HOWARTH *smiles slightly. He holds out his hand for* DONALD's
exercise book. DONALD *takes it out of his satchel and sits.*

HOWARTH (*looks at the exercise book*). Well, we wouldn't say,
would we, that the sun was about to go to bed, even if the
French do. What do we say?

DONALD. Mmm – it . . . (*Thinks.*) . . . sinks.

HOWARTH. Or sets, or goes down. Mmm-huh, well, all right,
but you don't really, do you? 'Mount' a hill – I mean, one
mounts a horse in English and that's about all these days.
What do you do to a hill?

JOANNA *looks for her scissors in her work basket.*

DONALD. Oh, climb it.

HOWARTH. Yeah. You see, you're still being a little lazy, really.
(JOANNA *looks in a tin on the piano. It rattles.*) When you know
what a word is – I mean, its literal translation – then think
from that to the word we'd use. Do you see? . . . So. Mmm-huh,
a little *wave*, a little grey *wave* on the horizon?

DONALD. Cloud, I mean. (*Laughs.*)

JOANNA *goes into the bedroom, opens and shuts a drawer in
the desk.*

HOWARTH. 'Course you do, it's common sense. He's standing
on top of a hill and he's looking across the plains, so even if the
first word that comes to mind is a wave, then think about it.
What is a wave, by the way?

DONALD. Um, um, um . . .

JOANNA *returns. Opens a drawer in the shelf unit. Looks in a
tin which rattles.*

HOWARTH. We had it just the other day.

DONALD. Um, orage. Orage.

HOWARTH. L'orage is the storm. (*Correcting his pronunciation.*)
Well, it was in that piece – and it sounds – (*breaks off as*
JOANNA *rattles the tins again*) – sounds roughly like, um . . .

(*Turns, looks at* JOANNA, *who has opened the tin, is looking inside it.*) No?

DONALD. It's um, um, um – (*Puts his hands to his face.*)

> HOWARTH *watches him.*

Vague. (*English pronunciation.*) Vague. (*French.*)

HOWARTH (*laughs*). Good boy!

> JOANNA *shuts the drawer, turns and goes out of the room.*

Now. (*Folds his hands, smiles at* DONALD.) Est-ce que vous voulez parler avec moi un peu, monsieur?

DONALD. Oui, monsieur. (*Tensely.*)

HOWARTH (*more relaxed*). Take it easy. Whoever does it with you, just imagine it's me, and we're amusing ourselves for a few minutes, mmm? This really *is* marks for jam. O.K.? Où habitez–vous?

DONALD. J'habite en Angleterre.

HOWARTH. D'accord. Vous vous apellez Donald Clenham et vous êtes de quelle nationalité?

DONALD. Anglais.

HOWARTH. Êtes vous sûr?

DONALD (*hesitates*). Oui, monsieur.

HOWARTH. Bon. Mais vos parents sont de quelle nationalité?

DONALD. Ma mère est anglais- (*Remembers the gender.*) -se, mais. mon père était . . . (*Pause, desperate guess.*) Eer-eesh.

HOWARTH. Irlandais.

DONALD. Irlandais.

HOWARTH. C'est ça que j'ai pensé. En ce cas, vous avez une imagination bizarre, non?

DONALD. Um – um –

HOWARTH. Bizarre, curious, extraordinary, extravagant. (*French.*) Bizarre! (DONALD *laughs.*) Mais, c'est vrai. Tous les Irlandais sont très imaginatifs, non? Et vous avez, vous-même, les yeux, les cheveux et la charme d'un irlandais, non? Est-ce que tu pense que tu as la charme d'un irlandais?

DONALD (*laughs*). Je l'espère.

HOWARTH. Et qu'est-ce que vous aimez faire, pour vous amuser?

DONALD. J'aime bien à chanter.

HOWARTH. Et vous chantez bien?

DONALD. No, sir ... Non, monsieur.

HOWARTH. Bien sùr, vous chantez bien. Tous les irlandais chantent bien parce qu'ils sont très sentimentaux.

JOANNA *enters.* HOWARTH *turns to her.*

Hello, I thought you were going to bed.

JOANNA. When I've finished your costume. (*Sits on the sofa.*)

HOWARTH. Why don't you leave it till the morning?

JOANNA. I'd rather find some other way of amusing myself in the morning, thank you.

HOWARTH. Well, I'm sorry it's such a job.

JOANNA. Well, it wouldn't be if you'd try it on.

HOWARTH. Well, I can't right now, can I?

JOANNA. Well, it would only take a moment.

HOWARTH (*turning to her irritably*). We're in the middle of some French.

JOANNA. Yes, I realize that, but as I've spent three hours sewing it together, I thought you might spare me thirty seconds trying it on. (*Pause, angrily.*) After which I'll take myself off to bed.

HOWARTH (*sharply*). O.K. ...

JOANNA. Oh, don't bother.

SHE *throws the robe on to the sofa and goes out.*

HOWARTH (*as she goes, making peace*). I don't mind ... (*Pause, turns to* DONALD.) Oh dear, I seem to have disgraced myself.

The door bell rings.

Oh, God! (*Goes off to answer the door.*)

MRS CLENHAM (*off*). Good evening, I'm Mrs Clenham, Donald's mother.

HOWARTH (*off*). Oh, come in.

MRS CLENHAM (*off*). I'm sorry to bother you like this.

DONALD, *recognizing his mother's voice, rises.*

HOWARTH (*enters, holding the door*). Donald, your mother.

MRS CLENHAM (*stepping in*). Pardon me for coming like this. I tried to contact you on the telephone but Les must have given me the wrong number. I brought some things over for – my son.

HOWARTH. Well, we're very glad to see you. I'll just tell my wife. (*Goes out, closes door, calls offstage.*) Darling!

MRS CLENHAM. Hello, Donnie.

DONALD. Hello, mum.

MRS CLENHAM (*in a low voice.*) Are you all right?

DONALD. Yes, I'm fine.

MRS CLENHAM. It was a bit of a shock, getting Les's message.

DONALD. I'm sorry, mum, I couldn't think how else to let you know. They . . . you know – it was a bit difficult.

MRS CLENHAM. Then Les giving me the wrong number . . . I dialled and dialled down at the shop, and I kept getting this man . . . he was very rude in the end. I was getting very worried.

DONALD. I'm sorry. (*Slightly irritable.*)

MRS CLENHAM. That's all right, Donnie. It doesn't matter. Anyway, you're all right then? It's very kind of them to ask you.

DONALD. Well, he's giving me a hand with revision – dictations and that. Right through. We were just in the middle of an oral.

MRS CLENHAM. Well, I'll be going straight back. (*Puts the brown paper carrier bag she has been carrying on a chair.*) Here, I've brought your pyjamas and tooth brush and your razor. (*Getting a cake-box out of the bag.*) And here's a cake. It's one of those orange gateaux.

DONALD (*looks down at the cake*). Oh.

MRS CLENHAM. You give it to them, Donnie, as you know them.

> HOWARTH and JOANNA *re-enter.*
> DONALD *puts the cake in the carrier bag, puts the bag on a chair.*

HOWARTH. Mrs Clenham, this is my wife. (*Shuts the door.*)

JOANNA. How do you do? (*They shake hands.*) Oh, do sit down. Would you like some tea or coffee or a drink?

MRS CLENHAM (*after a quick glance at* DONALD). No, thank you. There's a bus back in a minute, it's the last one.

JOANNA. Oh, what a shame you've got to rush off.

MRS CLENHAM. I'm sorry I came up so late, but it was difficult because Les gave me the wrong number. And then I didn't get his note until I was off in the evening from my work.

JOANNA. Oh, I see . . . what do you do?

MRS CLENHAM. Well, I'm at the Rex. At the Cinema.

DONALD *giggles nervously.*

(*After a glance at* DONALD.) I'm the usherette there.

JOANNA. Oh, I've always thought that must be lovely, seeing films as part of your work.

MRS CLENHAM. Oh yes, well most of them I see ten times in a week.

JOANNA. Yes, that must be a bit boring. (*Pause.*) Are you sure you haven't time to sit down?

MRS CLENHAM. No, thank you. I've got to get the bus. It's the last one. I just wanted to give my son some things.

JOANNA. I do hope you don't mind our stealing him for the weekend.

MRS CLENHAM. No, it's very kind of you to help him. (*Turns to* HOWARTH.) Thank you very much.

HOWARTH. Not at all. It's a pleasure.

MRS CLENHAM (*turning to* DONALD). Well, goodbye Donnie.

DONALD. Goodbye, mum.

MRS CLENHAM. And I'll be thinking of you on Monday.

DONALD. Thanks.

MRS CLENHAM (*crossing to* DONALD). Goodbye Donnie. (*Kisses him.*) And don't forget tomorrow's Sunday.

DONALD. No mum.

JOANNA. Why don't you walk your mother to the bus stop?

MRS CLENHAM. Well, it's very cold. You'll need your coat, Donnie.

c

DONALD. Yes, mum. (*Goes into the bedroom and collects his jacket.*)

MRS CLENHAM (*crossing towards* HOWARTH). Do you think he has a chance, then?

HOWARTH. Yes, yes, I certainly do.

MRS CLENHAM. But not certain to pass, then?

HOWARTH. Well, these things are slightly in the lap of the gods, unfortunately, Mrs Clenham. But we're doing our best.

> DONALD *returns, waits nervously.*

MRS CLENHAM. If anybody deserves to pass the exam and better his chances, Donnie does. He's not one for pushing himself forward, more's the pity. Of course I'm glad of that but he's . . .

DONALD (*a nervous laugh*). Yes, mum.

MRS CLENHAM. Well, thank you very much.

JOANNA. Not at all.

MRS CLENHAM. Thank you.

JOANNA. Good night.

MRS CLENHAM. Good night. (*Goes out.*)

DONALD (*to* HOWARTH, *out of nervousness*). Goodnight.

> DONALD *follows* MRS CLENHAM *out.*

HOWARTH. Well, there goes the lady who's responsible for the state of Donald's nerves. (*Laughs and watches* JOANNA *who is touching the costume.*) Shall I try that on as we seem to have a moment?

JOANNA. No thank you.

HOWARTH. Oh, come on, Jo.

> DONALD *enters, stays by the door, closes it.*

JOANNA (*to* DONALD). That was very quick.

DONALD. Um, she made me come back. She said it was too cold.

JOANNA. Oh, very wise. You can't afford to get anything now. Well, I'll leave you in peace.

> JOANNA *goes off and closes the door.* DONALD *comes to the table and sits.* HOWARTH *sits on the arm of the sofa.*

HOWARTH. I think we've done enough for one evening.

DONALD. Yes sir. (*Pause. Puts the book in his satchel.*) I'm sorry about that, sir.

HOWARTH. What? (*Looks at* DONALD.) About what?

DONALD. My mother. (*Pause.*) Her coming out here like that.

HOWARTH. But you've got nothing to apologise for. She just wanted to make sure you were all right.

DONALD. Yes sir. It's because she worries, sir.

HOWARTH. Yes, you've already told me that.

DONALD. Sir.

HOWARTH. Having parents is terribly difficult, one of the most difficult things in life – up to a certain age, anyway. Very few boys, in my quite extensive experience, aren't mortified by their mothers or their fathers or both, but they wouldn't feel mortified if there weren't a muddle of other feelings as well – protectiveness and, well, love and sheer irritation, which generally comes from vanity. We want those we love to be admired, and we feel for ourselves as well as for them when we suspect they aren't. (*Pause.*) From what I can make out, I think your mother is an admirable woman. (*Little pause.*) It must have been very hard for her.

DONALD (*nods, and in an emotional whisper*). I know that, sir.

HOWARTH. Yes, I'm sure you do.

> DONALD *nods again, emotionally.*

Mmmm. (*Little pause.*) By the way, tell me about our mutual friend, Les.

> DONALD *looks at him.*

Are you two very friendly?

DONALD. Well ... yes, well, as he's at Crabtree's and he lives near us and that –

HOWARTH. I got the *impression* you were quite close.

DONALD. Yes, well, I see him more than anyone else. He comes around in the evenings and we have lunch and that. (*Shrugs, smiles.*)

HOWARTH. Uh huh. You must like him then?

DONALD. Yes. (*Now slightly worried, and defensive.*) Well, he's all right. (*Little pause.*) We're going to go to France together next holidays.

HOWARTH. Really? What does your mother think about that?

DONALD. Well – (*Laughs.*) I haven't told her yet. She doesn't like Les too much. I think she quite likes him, but his parents are divorced – he lives with his mum – and as we're Catholics ...

HOWARTH. Ah, yes. I remember the business about the divorce. It was *one* of the reasons he left us – his mother took him away. His father was bad about maintenance, and Les had to go out to work. There are two little brothers, aren't there?

DONALD. Sisters.

HOWARTH. Yes, of course – it would be sisters. (*Smiles. Pours himself a whisky.*) What's he like now?

DONALD. Well, he's very nice. I mean, he's always, you know – helping me, doing things for me. Lots of times, things I don't even think about – or well, even need – you know, he does them.

HOWARTH. But you don't always enjoy it as much as you feel you ought to?

DONALD *looks at him, as if not understanding.*

DONALD. Sorry?

HOWARTH. I just mean that people – friends – sometimes get on our nerves, like parents. They do more than we want them to do.

DONALD. Well, once or twice – Once, I couldn't go into Crabtree's because mum hurt her back, and I had to take her to the doctor's, and Les, he thought I was just swinging it because he didn't know about mum, and he went around telling people I was ill, that he'd seen me the night before and I had a temperature with the 'flu. So, when I phoned up and said it was my mum that was ill, *they* thought I was swinging it too. But he was only trying to help, that's all.

HOWARTH. Were you angry?

DONALD. Well, he got a bit upset.

HOWARTH. So you apologised? (*Smiling.*)

DONALD. He was a bit upset. It didn't matter. I mean, I shouldn't have lost my temper.

HOWARTH. Why not? (*Pause.*) If he did something bloody silly and interfering ...

DONALD. I don't know. He takes it very hard.

HOWARTH. Les never told you about St Martin's?

DONALD. No, well, just that he was there.

HOWARTH. One of the reasons Les left St Martin's was because of the difficulty between his parents. But there was another reason. (DONALD *turns and looks at* HOWARTH.) He was getting – well, a little too fond of one of the other boys. He kept writing him letters – love letters, in fact – and generally behaving – desperately. The other boy took the letters to the Headmaster – at least, his parents did. They'd found them in his satchel, and the Head was – he's a kind man, but not the world's most proficient psychologist – and he was a little clumsy about the whole thing. Unfortunately – or from some points of view, perhaps, fortunately – Les's mother said she wanted to withdraw him while all this was going on, and the Head, who, as I've said is a kind enough creature, and normally under the circumstances would have done something to keep the boy on, let him go. So ... (*Looks at* DONALD.)

DONALD (*after a long pause, in horror*). D'you mean he's a homo?

HOWARTH. It's not the word I'd use – ever, no. But boys, particularly at that age, can be sexually very confused. They're as much homosexual from necessity as they're heterosexual in their – (*Gestures.*) – dreams. Mmm. The point, as far as their future happiness is concerned, is whether they grow out of it. The world, thank God, is learning not to judge homosexuals as if they were criminals. *But*, homosexual boys – men – (*Shrugs.*)

– do have a tendency to make emotional claims, to develop habits of dependence that can lead – if the other person is normal – to difficulties. Do you see?

DONALD *nods.*

Relationships in even the most ordinary of circumstances can be difficult enough, God knows – (*Laughs.*) – *and* depend upon habits. Joanna and I have the dieting thing, for example. It doesn't mean very much – at least, as far as actual eating goes – but it's become a familiar part of our lives, a habit that's a kind of reassurance, really. All right, but other habits – and in less ordinary circumstances – habits, say, where Les makes a nuisance of himself – like that little business at Crabtree's, because he's possessive, well, cares too intensely, let's say, and then gets too upset when you're quite rightly irritated, so that *you* apologise – that sounds a little too like a marriage to me. You might be drawn in further than you want. I'm only telling you all this because at school it's a part of my job, perhaps the most important part, to pass on what little information my experience has given me – and because you said you and Les were going to Paris together – perhaps I shouldn't have told you this – I thought I ought to warn you about possible complications. I certainly don't want you to do anything more than think about it all.

DONALD (*pause*). I didn't know about that, – about Les, sir – except my having to apologise to him all the time. I mean, that used to get on my nerves, but I didn't know about that.

HOWARTH (*pats* DONALD'*s arm, relaxed*). Oh, don't worry. I know you like girls. (*Smiling.*)

DONALD. Sir?

HOWARTH. Well, you do like girls, don't you? I know you like looking at them.

DONALD *laughs, looks at him; is overcome with embarrassment.*

I'm trying to be exquisitely tactful – (*Takes out of his pocket the folded picture.*) – and return your property to you without a fuss. It fell out of your satchel in all your comings and goings this morning.

DONALD. No, it's not mine, sir.

HOWARTH. Oh, Donald. Come on, take it. I know it's yours.

DONALD *goes to take it.*

Just a minute, there's something you can explain to me – (*Takes the picture back, opens it out.*) – the boots. What's the appeal of the boots? (*Points to them.*) The rest of it gets to me, in my own thin-blooded way. Proud breasts, pertly up-tilted – (*Tracing lines with his finger.*) – saucy little nipples, suave hips, an exciting sheen on her flanks and a vee of shadows, which is what she wears instead of pubic hair. I always wonder whether it's rubbed out on the negative or shaved off before they take the photo. But the boots – what's the appeal of the boots?

DONALD *stares down, transfixed ... makes a giggling noise.*

Mmmm? (*Smiles slowly, then laughs.*)

DONALD *also laughs.*

It's not fair. I know exactly what the appeal of the boots is. Here. (*Hands the photo back to* DONALD.) The real thing, of course, is trickier. It tends not to go about nude in boots, with all the embarrassing bits removed – unless you specifically ask it to – and it's very much in love with you. The real thing tends to be hairily human, with all that that implies.

The door opens. JOANNA *comes in in dressing gown and slippers.*

Et voilà, c'est tout pour ce soir, Monsieur Clenham.

JOANNA. And high time. If Donald's going to keep fit for Monday morning, he'd better get his sleep.

DONALD *gets up, carries his satchel into the bedroom, leaving the door open.*

HOWARTH. Goodnight!

JOANNA. Goodnight!

> DONALD *puts his satchel down on the desk in the bedroom and returns to the main room.*

DONALD. Oh, my things. (*Collects his mother's carrier bag from the chair.*)

JOANNA. You do know where the bathroom is?

> DONALD *goes to take the cake-box out, half-lifts it from the bag, then, too embarrassed to give it to* JOANNA, *puts it back and hurries out of the main door.*

I'm a bitch. I've been brooding in my bath and you are a terribly good teacher, aren't you?

HOWARTH. Quite good.

JOANNA (*hand on his shoulder*). And it's because you're all the things I blame you for – a liar, self-indulgent, lovable, sexy and exhibitionist.

HOWARTH. Am I lovable?

JOANNA (*caresses his head*). Well, quite lovable. But you're very lovable with him. I admit it. He's not very bright, is he?

HOWARTH. No, not very.

JOANNA. And you make him brighter than he is, which must be one of the gifts of a teacher.

> HOWARTH *points ruefully to the pile of exercise books and reaches for one.*

Oh you're not, are you?

HOWARTH. Darling, I've got to.

> *Pause.* HOWARTH *starts correcting the exercises.*

JOANNA. Do you think I'm more like a flower or a cow? I've been reading novels about pregnant ladies, and when they're written by men, we're languid and dream-like, curiously beautiful, in touch with the mystery and other balls about creation. Our faces open as flowers, etc., etc., but when they're written by other ladies, especially the ones with degrees, we're always cow-like, sow-like, lumpish and clumsy. Which do you think I'm like?

HOWARTH. Mmmm?

JOANNA. Cow, sow or flower?

HOWARTH. Flower.

JOANNA. A flower with a urine test on Monday. You know, that Doctor Lafflin treats my bottom half like his wife's handbag, and my top half like an idiot son – but he does accept my little glass jar with a twinkle. The only time he's at all personal, is when he twinkles at me, and as I'm either holding or have just handed him a glass of my pee, I can scarcely twinkle back at him, can I, without seeming insane or obscene. Which do you think I am? Insane or obscene?

HOWARTH. You're not insane.

DONALD *comes back in, wearing pyjamas and slippers and carrying the bag and a pile of his clothes with the cake-box on top. He smiles at* HOWARTH *and* JOANNA *and goes in to the bedroom, puts his clothes on a chair.*

JOANNA. What has he got in that cake-box?

DONALD *turns on his bedroom light.* JOANNA *goes to the bedroom door and knocks.*

DONALD (*puts the cake-box on top of the folded bed*). Yes?

JOANNA. Donald? Are you all right in there? Got everything?

DONALD. Um, yes, thank you. It's very nice.

JOANNA. Good.

DONALD (*coming into the main room*). The only thing is – um – is there a bed?

JOANNA *and* HOWARTH *laugh and* JOANNA *goes in to the bedroom, followed by* DONALD. HOWARTH *follows to the door.*

JOANNA. I'm so sorry, it's all made up. It only takes a second.

JOANNA *hands the carry-cot to* DONALD *who puts it against the wall.*

I'm sorry about all the baby stuff, I was afraid you'd take all the nappies and rubber knickers as a joke in bad taste. (*Hands the cake-box to* DONALD, *takes the cover off the folded bed and wheels it into the centre of the bedroom.*) It opens this way –

DONALD *puts the cake-box on the chest of drawers, unfolds the bed, which is ready made up.* JOANNA *puts away the bed-cover and brings out a rug.*

HOWARTH (*stepping forward to help*). Can you manage?

DONALD. Yes thank you, sir.

JOANNA. Donald, you're to stop calling him 'Sir'. You're a guest, and besides, it ages me.

HOWARTH. Yes, we're Richard and Joanna from now on.

JOANNA. Now, is that all right then? There's an extra blanket if you want it.

HOWARTH *goes out of the room and sits at the table again,* JOANNA *follows.* DONALD *straightens the rug on the bed then comes into main room.*

DONALD. Um – the only thing – is there a church?

HOWARTH. Yes, there is. St Mark's – it's next door to the Post Office, a one-minute walk.

DONALD. Oh yes, I saw it.

JOANNA. What time have you to be there?

DONALD. Well, seven o'clock.

JOANNA. Seven!

DONALD. Well, I could go to the eleven o'clock mass, I suppose.

JOANNA. Is that all right? Lovely. We'll remember.

DONALD. Um, well, goodnight, sir. Goodnight, Mrs . . .

JOANNA. You've forgotten already!

DONALD (*with difficulty*). 'Night then, Richard. Goodnight . . .

JOANNA. Joanna.

DONALD. Goodnight, Joanna.
JOANNA. Goodnight, Donald.

> DONALD *goes into the bedroom and closes the door. He turns out the light and gets into bed.*

JOANNA. And what about you? I've suddenly realized I'm very neurotic, and only a cuddle will cure me.
HOWARTH (*having turned back to his exercises*). Say half an hour?
JOANNA. That's no use to me. I'll be asleep in three minutes, as you well know. Give me one now, on account.

> HOWARTH *turns and draws her to him. He cuddles her.*

JOANNA. Mmm, well, all right, if you promise to cuddle me if I'm asleep. I need some basic soothing.
HOWARTH. I promise.
JOANNA. Mmm. (*Suspiciously, goes towards the door.*) 'Night, Richard. (*Imitating* DONALD.)

> HOWARTH *looks after her, then goes back to his exercise book, then gets up. He goes to the hatch, brings out the biscuit tin, takes about four biscuits out. He sits down, takes a biscuit and continues to mark the exercise book.*
> *The lights dim to suggest the passing of about half an hour, then the one light by* HOWARTH's *table up, and* HOWARTH *still marking.*
> DONALD, *from his bedroom, has begun a low, keening sound. He is sitting up hunched together and rocking backwards and forwards in his sleep.* HOWARTH, *at first not noticing, goes on working. The keening noises get louder.* HOWARTH *looks up, looks at* DONALD's *bedroom door, as the stage fills with the noise.*
> HOWARTH *gets to his feet, goes to the bedroom door.*

HOWARTH (*knocks*). Donald, Donald. Are you all right?

> *The noise stops, then starts again.*

(*Opening the door and turning on the light – tenderly.*) What's the matter? Are you all right?

> HOWARTH *goes into the bedroom, bends over the bed, gently pushes* DONALD *back onto the pillow.* DONALD *stops moaning and sinks back, still asleep.* HOWARTH *straightens the blanket.*

All right then, there you are. There. Now go to sleep. (*Comes back to the door, is about to shut it.*)

DONALD (*in a strange voice, intimately insolent*). 'Night, Richard.

> HOWARTH *stands with his hand on the knob, then turns out the light and closes the door gently.*

CURTAIN

ACT TWO

Scene One

The Howarth living-room. The following morning.
In the bedroom the bed has been made neatly and a chair from the desk has been placed by the door.
The action starts in the living-room. DONALD *is sitting at the table, pen in hand, exercise book before him.* HOWARTH *is standing by the window, the dictation text-book in his hand.*

HOWARTH. And you say you can't remember it?

DONALD. Um, I don't think so.

HOWARTH. Sure?

DONALD. Yes.

HOWARTH. Mm. I must have done it at school. Right – I'll read it through again – by the way – (*Smiling.*) – did you sleep well?

DONALD (*looks at him, slight pause, almost apprehensive*). Yes, thank you, um, Richard.

HOWARTH. You gave me quite a turn.

    DONALD *looks at him, smiling awkwardly.*

(*Smiling.*) Don't you remember?

    DONALD *shakes his head.*

You were – I don't know what you were doing. Keening.

DONALD. I – I'm sorry.

HOWARTH. Don't be silly. There's nothing to be sorry about – but did you know you do it?

DONALD. Well, sometimes I – I – make this noise, mum says.

HOWARTH. Actually it's very effective – quite eerie. (*Pause, as* DONALD *looks down, mortified.*) Have you ever seen anyone about it? A doctor?

DONALD. I think mum mentioned it once to, um, Father O'Toole.

HOWARTH. And what did he say?

DONALD. That I'd grow out of it.

HOWARTH (*little pause*). Then just when I thought I got you quieted – (*Smiling.*) – you said, with a really quite unnerving lucidity, ''Night, Richard.' You don't remember that, either?

DONALD *shakes his head.*

(*Laughs.*) It actually chilled my blood. (*Laughs.*)
You sounded so – accomplished. Well, I'll read it through again. Ready?

DONALD *nods. As* HOWARTH *reads, he runs his pen along the top of the lines.*

'Ce matin-là Jean avait parlé beaucoup des blès et de ce qu'il appelait la "culture intensive", mais il ne possédait aucune notion sérieuse d'agriculture. (*Looks up sharply.*) D'agriculture. (*Repeating it, with a slightly knowing exaggeration.*) Félicie haussait parfois les épaules. Philibert – (*Looks at* DONALD.) – jetait de temps en temps vers elle un regard de sympathie, et une fois il avait chucoté: – "Ne vous fachez . . ."

JOANNA *comes in, goes to the sofa for her handbag. She smiles at* HOWARTH. *He smiles back at her. She looks in her handbag.*

'"Ne vous fachez pas. Votre frère dit des bêtises, mais cela fait passer le temps." Mais Félicie l'arrêta . . .'

JOANNA *makes an apologetic gesture, goes over to the shelf and picks up a bunch of keys.*

'Mais Félicie . . .' (*Stops.*)

JOANNA. Sorry, darling. I'm going to try and get a cup of coffee from the Haywards. I'll be back at lunch-time. The joint's on.

HOWARTH. O.K. See you then.

JOANNA *smiles at* DONALD, *who smiles back, withdraws.*

'Mais Félicie l'arrêta court. Chut! Faîtes-moi donc le plaisir de vous occuper de ce qui vous regarde!' (*Sound of door closing.* HOWARTH *glances out of the window.*) 'Elle s'était mise en colère. Elle était bonne mais vive, et toujours prête à s'emporter . . .' (*Waves out of the window.*) '. . . à s'emporter, surtout quand il s'agissait de sa famille.' O.K.?

DONALD *nods.*

(*Saunters towards him.*) You didn't make any corrections, did you?

DONALD. No.

HOWARTH (*leans over him, runs his finger rapidly along the lines*). You were quite right not to. Well, that's very good, isn't it? Except for this. One little mistake. But otherwise very good. (*Pause.*) Well done.

DONALD. Well – it seemed easy – I don't know why.

HOWARTH. Don't you? (*Pleasantly, with a hint of underlying menace.*) Really? Probably just a matter of confidence, eh?

DONALD *nods.*

(*Pointing at the exercise book.*) Of course, your little mistake was a stupid one. '*Une* fois'–not only did I say it quite distinctly, but you *know* perfectly well that 'fois' is feminine.

DONALD. Well, um, that's meant to be an 'e' there. (*Points.*) It's just spludged.

HOWARTH. So it is. Well, that makes it perfect. Something to be proud of. Could you stand doing another? A very short one.

DONALD (*nods*). The only thing is – (*In a mumble.*) – I'm supposed to be in church.

HOWARTH (*as if not having heard, overlapping* DONALD's *speech*). No, I think you'll find all these too easy. Have a go at this. Just a few lines – no splodges, mind. (*Smiles.*)

DONALD *sits listening.* HOWARTH *recites from memory.*

'Ange plein de gaieté, connaissez-vous l'angoisse,
La honte, les remords, les sanglots, les ennuis
Et les vagues terreurs de ces affreuses nuits
Qui compriment le coeur comme un papier qu'on froisse?
Ange plein de gaieté, connaissez-vous l'angoisse?

'Ange plein de beauté, connaissez-vous les rides,
Et la peur de vieillir, et ce hideux tourment
De lire la secrète horreur du dévoument
Dans des yeux ou longtemps burent nos yeux avides?
Ange plein de beauté, connaissez-vous les rides?'

OK? (*Looks at* DONALD, *who has clearly not understood a word.*)

DONALD. Well . . . (*Shrugs.*)

HOWARTH. Have a go, anyway.

> HOWARTH *speaks at dictation speed, pausing between every two or three words.*

'Ange plein de gaieté, connaissez-vous l'angoisse,
La honte, les remords, les sanglots, les ennuis
Et les vagues terreurs de ces affreuses nuits
Qui compriment le coeur comme un papier qu'on froisse?'

> DONALD *writes, clearly completely confused, shaking his head.*

Am I going too fast?

DONALD. No.

HOWARTH. Good.
'Ange plein de gaieté, connaissez-vous l'angoisse?'
How's it going?

DONALD. Well, not really – (*Laughs nervously.*)

HOWARTH. Well, perhaps I'd better stop there. Eh? Look through it then.

> DONALD *does so.*

'Ange plein de gaieté, connaissez-vous l'angoisse,
La honte, les remords, les sanglots, les ennuis . . .

(Crosses the room, looking down at DONALD's *attempt to do the dictation.)*

'Et les vagues terreurs de ces affreuses nuits
Qui compriment le coeur . . .'

DONALD *abandons the attempt, sits staring blankly down at his book.*

'. . . comme un papier qu'on froisse?
Ange plein de gaieté, connaissez-vous l'angoisse?'

Pause. DONALD *looks at* HOWARTH.

Well?

DONALD. I, um, got a bit lost.

HOWARTH. Could you understand it?

DONALD. Well, some of it.

HOWARTH. Then translate what you've got, and see if you can work backwards, filling in the blanks, so to speak. Not exactly examination practice, but a test of your – um . . . *(Gestures.)*

DONALD. Well, that'd take a bit of time.

HOWARTH *(looks at him)*. We've *got* time.

HOWARTH *picks up a newspaper from the sofa and stands by* DONALD, *reading.* DONALD *stares at his exercise book, rocking backwards and forwards slightly as he did in his sleep.* HOWARTH *turns back to look out of the window.*

DONALD *bends over his exercise book helplessly, picks up his pen, frowns, scratches down some words, shaking his head, shrugging, then looks towards* HOWARTH.

HOWARTH *pays no attention.* DONALD *writes down a few more words. There is a long pause,* DONALD *staring towards* HOWARTH.

HOWARTH. Well?

DONALD. Well, I got some of the words . . . *(In a mumble.)*

HOWARTH. Mmm – huh. *(Picks up* DONALD's *exercise book.)*
  'Ange' – hip. My pronunciation must be a joke. 'Hanche' – hip.

D

'Ange' – (*Drawing the word out.*) – angel. (*Laughs again.*) Your first sentence appears to read, then, 'Hip plan of the limp' – 'limp?' – oh, I see. (*Laughs.*) 'Gaieté' – gait – limp – ingenious, 'do you know,' 'connaissez-vous,' *well* done, – 'l'angoisse' 'the English' – Didn't you even grasp, from its rhythms and rhymes, that it was a poem?

> DONALD *shakes his head.* HOWARTH *takes down a copy of* Les Fleurs du Mal, *opens it at the poem 'Réversibilité' and puts it down contemptuously in front of* DONALD.

Look at it.

> DONALD *does.*

(*Pointing out each word.*) Literally – 'Angel, full of gaiety, do you know the anguish, the shame, the remorse, the sobs, the tedium and the vague' – what did you put for 'vagues'?

DONALD (*in a mumble*). Um, 'waves'. (*Starts to weep.*)

HOWARTH. Of course. 'The tedium and the *vague* terrors of those frightful nights which compress the heart like a paper that one crumples. Angel, full of gaiety, do you know the anguish?' Mmmm? There's only one word there, actually, that you don't know – 'froisser' – to restrain or crumple – eh? There are no grammatical difficulties?

> DONALD *shakes his head.*

And the fact that it's a painfully beautiful *poem* shouldn't have worried *you*, should it? As you didn't *register* it was a poem?

> DONALD *shakes his head.* DONALD *stares at him, puts his hands to his eyes. There is a silence.*

Well – do you think I'm being unfair?

> DONALD *shakes his head.*

HOWARTH (*with his back to him, still looking out of the window*). Do you think I'm being cruel?

> DONALD *shakes his head.*

Well, I am. And do you know why? (*Turns around.*)

DONALD *shakes his head.*

(*Crossing to* DONALD.) Oh yes you do. (*Leans across, picks up* DONALD's *exercise book, flicks back through it, hands it to* DONALD.) What's this?

DONALD (*after a pause*). That dictation, sir.

HOWARTH. I do five of these a week, so it's scarcely surprising that I can't remember which I've done with whom. But *you* remembered, didn't you? From the first sentence. (*Little pause.*) Didn't you?

DONALD *sits hunched, looking down.*

Didn't you? Mmm?

DONALD. Sir.

HOWARTH. Because you wanted me to give you good marks? (*Contemptuously.*)

DONALD *shakes his head.*

Because you wanted to impress me?

DONALD (*after a pause, in a mumble*). Sir.

HOWARTH. But it's cheating. And that's a very serious matter. (*Gently.*) I don't mean cheating *me*, about which I care not one damn, but cheating yourself, about which I do care. Don't you see?

DONALD. Sir.

HOWARTH. You don't have to impress *me* with anything. At least, not in this way – that's something one keeps for one's girl-friend, or whatever.

DONALD *weeps, uncontrollably.*

Even so, I was unfair, wasn't I?

DONALD *shakes his head.*

I think I was insulted, and the very last thing you wanted to do was insult me. In fact, you wanted me to praise you – and what, after all, could be more flattering than that? Mmmm? (*Very gently.*) *Donald?*

DONALD *goes on looking down, crying.*

Donald. (*Pause.*) *Donald.*

DONALD *looks up slowly.*

I'm sorry. (*Smiling.*)

DONALD (*his voice shaking*). Sorry, sir.

HOWARTH. No, you're not to be. Not now. And the 'sir' you already know about.

DONALD *looks up, attempts to smile at* HOWARTH'S *smile.*

Donald, you do worry me, you know.

DONALD *begins to say* 'sir', *checks himself.*

You're very attractive – my wife says you are – and you're not at all stupid, although I think you think you are, and you laugh – when you laugh, which is not nearly often enough – terribly nicely. But you give off an impression of – what? – well, as if you're permanently frightened. (*Pause.*) You are, aren't you?

DONALD (*in a whisper*). Yes.

HOWARTH. Of me?

DONALD (*looks down*). Yes.

HOWARTH. But not badly frightened of me? At least, not frightened in a bad way?

DONALD *shakes his head.*

Well, that sounds about right. (*Laughs.*) But your trouble is – may I tell you what the trouble is?

DONALD *nods. Looks at* HOWARTH.

Your trouble is not that you're frightened but that you don't realise that, on the whole, other people are frightened too, you see. They are. Always. Why, I'm even a little frightened of you.

DONALD *looks at him, laughs slightly.*

But I am. I expect you judge me, don't you, in the way that we half-consciously judge *everyone* we know. Perhaps you find me pompous, silly, boring, fat? A trifle fat? Anyway, putting on weight?

DONALD *sniffs and laughs simultaneously.*

But I am. Joanna tells me, and I feel it, other people – my students – must notice it. Well, that doesn't matter – there are other things I could be judged for – humiliated because of – just like you. That's the point, you see. But where I have a slight edge over you is that I know that other people are as frightened as I am. Of being found out. We all are. It's the great human secret. Do you believe me?

DONALD *is staring at him as if hypnotized.*

But perhaps we go some way towards overcoming it by talking of it. Perhaps you and I needn't be more than a necessary little bit frightened of each other again? (*Smiling.*) Eh? (*Little pause.*) How do you feel?

DONALD *looks at him, looks down, there is a long pause, begins to cry again very slightly.*

You're not unhappy, are you?

DONALD *shakes his head.* HOWARTH *puts his hand on* DONALD's *shoulder.*

You're not crying though, are you?

DONALD *shakes his head, puts his arm to his eyes.* HOWARTH *goes over to* DONALD, *puts his arm around his shoulder.*

Donald, don't.

DONALD *sits, his arm still over his eyes.*

(HOWARTH *removes his arm gently.*) Got a handkerchief?

DONALD (*fumbles in his pocket, takes out a handkerchief, blows his nose, wipes his eyes, draws a breath, then in a brave, trembling voice*). I'm sorry.

HOWARTH. You're not to say sorry to me – ever again. People who say sorry all the time are simply doing dirt on themselves, mmm?

> JOANNA *opens the door, comes in, stops.* HOWARTH *steps away from* DONALD. DONALD *blows his nose.*

JOANNA. I'm sorry. (*Little pause.*) Only it's gone eleven. (*She is carrying a basket of shrubs.*)

HOWARTH. Gone eleven?

JOANNA. Donald's church.

HOWARTH. My God. (*Looks at* DONALD.) I completely forgot.

DONALD. Um, it doesn't matter, it was my fault.

JOANNA (*advancing into the room*). Well, hadn't he better get along. He won't be too late. (*Goes on out of the door, leaving it open.*)

> DONALD *looks at* HOWARTH.

HOWARTH. All right? (*In a low voice.*)

> DONALD *nods and fetches his coat from the bedroom.*

O.K. See you then. (*Smiles.*)

> DONALD *goes out.* HOWARTH *stands for a moment, looking towards the door, then goes over to it.* JOANNA *comes in, carrying two vases.*

(*Taking one from her.*) Here, let me.

> He takes the larger of the two vases from her and places it on the table. JOANNA *closes the door and puts the smaller vase on a stool.*

How are you, then?

JOANNA (*busy*). Preg-nant.

HOWARTH. Poor darling. How were Peter and Sally?

JOANNA. Out.

HOWARTH. Out?

JOANNA. Yes. Not in. (*Takes the vase* HOWARTH *has placed on the table over to one by the window.*)

HOWARTH. Well, it looks as if we have the house to ourselves for a change. (*Goes over to the table, starts arranging the books.*) What shall we do?

> JOANNA *goes over to the sofa.*

JOANNA. Peel. Peel the potatoes. Top and tail. The sprouts. In a minute. (*She picks up the other vase of flowers and takes them into the lounge.*)

HOWARTH. Poor darling. Can I help?

JOANNA. What was that all about?

HOWARTH. What all about?

JOANNA. In here. Between you two. He was crying, wasn't he?

HOWARTH. Yes. I was a little tactless. I pushed him a bit harder than I meant to.

JOANNA. I see. (*Little pause.*) Does it happen often?

HOWARTH. Happen often?

JOANNA. With your other boys. At school.

HOWARTH. With my other boys?

JOANNA (*sharper*). You're developing an extraordinary trick of repeating all my questions. Did you know?

HOWARTH. Well, you're asking some extraordinary questions. Did you know?

> There is a pause. JOANNA *looking at the Sunday paper,* HOWARTH *looking at her.*

Well, what do you mean, happen often? If you mean, do I usually reduce my boys to tears, the answer is no, I most certainly do not. If you mean, is there occasional tension between us, the answer is yes, when the other party is someone like Donald. (*Little pause.* JOANNA *puts down the paper and listens.*) There *have* been tears in my time. As in the time of any schoolmaster, I should think. The boys are vulnerable and the masters impatient. The resulting concussion is – sometimes – unpleasant. It's one of the hazards of the profession. It generally means I lose a perfectly clean handkerchief, as I did with Donald. (*Little pause.*) As a matter of fact, I merely caught him doing something silly – a kind of useless cheating – and nagged at him because of it more than I should have, and his – his nerve broke. Not his strongest point at the best of times, as his 'mum' warned us. It was my fault. And I said so. (*Little pause.*) I feel upset enough about it, you needn't worry. And I particularly dislike showing myself a brutal bungler in front of you. O.K.?

JOANNA (*looks at him – there is a pause*). Come here.

HOWARTH. What?

JOANNA. Come on. Please. O.K.?

> HOWARTH *goes over,* JOANNA *takes his hand, raises it to her lips, kisses it.*

HOWARTH (*sits on the sofa with his arm round her*). Have you noticed it's when people apologise to each other that the tears come?

JOANNA (*gives him a kiss*). I'm sorry.

HOWARTH (*gently, after a moment*). But where are the tears?

JOANNA. Oh, I can manage them if you want?

HOWARTH. No thanks. (*Indicates* DONALD's *door.*) Enough is as good as a feast.

JOANNA. Feast? With all those biscuits inside you? (*Prods his stomach.*)

HOWARTH. I – (*Laughs.*) We had a sort of elevenses.

JOANNA. Give us a kiss, pig.

> HOWARTH *does so, then straightens up.*

But why should he cheat?

HOWARTH. What? (*Shrugs.*) Why do boys ever cheat? Because it's easier than not.

JOANNA. But it's not an examination or anything. Why should he cheat with you?

HOWARTH. Well, I don't know, I suppose because he wanted to get a good mark, I suppose. Or for his self-esteem, which, God knows, needs boosting.

JOANNA. You mean, to win your approval?

HOWARTH. Not mine necessarily – at least, not personally. Probably just because his nerve is weak – and it's not tested when you do well.

JOANNA. Perhaps his nerve is weak because his feelings are strong. He wanted *you* to respect him – after all, if he cries when *you* find him out –

HOWARTH. Well, I expect I'm the only teacher ever to take the mildest interest. (*Sits at the table.*) The question is, what would he have done if Father O'Toole had caught him cheating? (*Starts to mark exercise books.*)

JOANNA (*looks at him*). When I was out, I suddenly got frightened. (HOWARTH *turns to her.*) I didn't go to the Haywards at all.

HOWARTH (*looking at her anxiously*). Oh, why not?

JOANNA. It was stupid, but I suddenly remembered the last time I went – (*Swings her legs off, looks at* HOWARTH.) – and Sally talked all the time of her forceps delivery – did you know Tom was a forceps – they caught his head with the forceps and tugged it out. Although you wouldn't think so to look at him now – his head's enormous. This last week all I can think about is what could go wrong.

HOWARTH. But you're supremely healthy – everyone keeps saying so.

JOANNA. Yes, but is he? Or she? Or – I don't know. I don't know if I'm up to what every woman's meant to fulfil herself in. The Americans just put you under about a week before, and you wake up with a baby or two, all sluiced down and probably gift-wrapped. (*Stands up.*) God, I'm boring. You've no idea how nervy I feel, from how boring I sound. (*Bends*

down with a sigh, turns on the radio. It is Bach. She smiles at
HOWARTH, *goes out.*)

HOWARTH (*listens to the music, then goes to the door, shouting*).
Darling – you're not at all boring.

JOANNA (*returning*). Sprouts or peas?

> HOWARTH *goes over to her, kisses her on the cheek, cuddles her.*

Peas or sprouts?

HOWARTH (*they kiss, he laughs*). Both, possibly?

JOANNA. All right, but you do the potatoes then. The elephant
and the pig. (*As she does a few steps of a lumbering dance.*)

> *There is a ring at the door-bell, only just audible.* JOANNA
> *looks at her watch.*

Back already? I always heard that was the Catholic system –
little but often. (*Goes out.*)

> HOWARTH *returns to the table.*
> *Sound of voices, then footsteps.*

(*Enters with* LES.) Darling – a friend of Donald's – Les.

LES. Sir.

HOWARTH. Oh – (*Getting up.*) – hello. (*Little pause.*) I'm afraid
Donald's out – he's gone to church.

LES. Oh, I thought he'd go to the early morning mass – he
usually –

JOANNA. We've been corrupting him, I'm afraid. We always
sleep late on Sundays.

> *There is a pause.*

(*Glances at* HOWARTH, *puzzled, then back to* LES.) Anyway,
do sit down.

LES. Oh, well, thank you. (*Sits down.*)

HOWARTH (*still standing*). Um, well, you cycled, did you?

LES. Yes. (*Little pause.*) I wasn't sure what time you meant me
to come exactly, you said coffee or tea and I thought that's
either eleven or in the afternoon. (*Laughs.*)

HOWARTH (*to* JOANNA). Um, I suggested to Les that if he should
  be cycling this way today, he look Donald up. They were going
  for a ride together yesterday.

JOANNA. But if you cycled, you must be exhausted.

LES. No, I'm used to it, we go out every week almost.

  There is a pause.

HOWARTH. That's two of your rides I seem to have messed up.

LES. Oh, it doesn't matter. We can go next week. Well – (*Makes
  as if to rise.*)

JOANNA. Darling, what about a drink? Or would you prefer tea
  or coffee, Les?

LES. No, well, that's all right, thank you very much.

JOANNA. Well, *I'd* like a drink.

  HOWARTH *goes to the door, shuts it, goes over to the shelf,
  pours a sherry, brings it back, gives it to* JOANNA.

You work in Crabtree's too, do you?

LES. Yes, in the cutlery.

JOANNA. Oh, really? I tried to get some spoons there once, but
  they were so expensive.

LES. Yes, I know. I always tell people to try somewhere else.

JOANNA (*laughs*). Like Woolworths?

LES. Yes. (*They both laugh.*)

JOANNA (*taking her drink*). Darling, I'm sure Les could be
  persuaded. Have a *small* sherry – you know it makes sense.

LES. Oh, well – thanks very much.

  HOWARTH, *after a fractional hesitation, pours* LES *a very
  small sherry.*

JOANNA. Have you known Donald long?

LES. Well, since just after I left school.

JOANNA. You weren't at school together, then?

HOWARTH. No, actually Les was at St Martin's for a short time.

JOANNA. Really?

HOWARTH (*handing* LES *his drink*). Although we scarcely knew each other.

LES. Yes, I was only there two years, I had to leave early.

JOANNA. Oh? (*Interrogatively.*)

HOWARTH. Which is how he came to miss me.

LES. That was one of my regrets. (*With sudden intensity.*)

JOANNA. How very flattering. (*To* HOWARTH.)

HOWARTH. Yes. (*Laughs.*) The best way to keep one's reputation is not to have it put to the test.

LES. Everybody at school said you were marvellous and – well, Don says the same.

JOANNA. I must have more of this – hang on a minute. (*Goes out.*)

HOWARTH (*after a pause*). Well, I'm sorry Donald isn't here, after all your exertions.

LES. He'll be gone a long time then, will he?

HOWARTH. I don't know how long these things last – but I'm afraid I'll have to do a bit of French with him –

LES. Oh, I see.

HOWARTH. He's getting such a lot done – I'm terrified of breaking the spell. (*Little pause.*) I'm sorry.

LES (*finishes his drink*). No, it doesn't. (*Shakes his head, gets up.*) Well, perhaps I might as well get back anyway.

HOWARTH. Well, at least you've got the weather, mmm?

LES *looks at him uncertainly.*

Still, I'm glad you could drop in.

JOANNA (*comes back in*). Oh, you're not going?

LES. Well, I've got to get on.

JOANNA. Oh, what a shame.

HOWARTH. Les wants to get as much of the sun as he can.

JOANNA. Well, it's been *very* nice . . . (*Holds out her hand.*)

LES. Oh, well, thank you. (*They shake hands.*)

As they do, there is the sound of the door closing, footsteps.

JOANNA. Ah!

DONALD *comes in, stops when he sees* LES.

LES. Hello, Don.

JOANNA. You got back just in time. That was lucky.

DONALD. Well, there wasn't an eleven o'clock mass.

JOANNA. Oh dear, I am sorry. Let's all sit down again, at least, and have another drink.

LES. Oh, well, thanks, but if you're going to be working? (*Looks at* HOWARTH.)

JOANNA. Surely you're not going to do anything before lunch?

HOWARTH. Um, no, no, not now – (*Looks at his watch.*) – I shouldn't think. Do have a drink.

JOANNA. Do sit down. (LES *sits down again*, HOWARTH *pours a sherry for* DONALD.) Les was just telling us that he never got to do French with Richard at St Martin's.

LES. Of course we don't need French at Crabtree's – (*Contemptuously.*) – but we're going to France next holiday – and now Don'll have to do all the talking, eh, Don?

JOANNA. To France? How exciting!

HOWARTH *gives* DONALD *his sherry.*

LES. Yes, we thought we'd take our bikes, you know, just put them on the boat and then sort of cycle off – we thought we might even get to Paris, eh, Don?

DONALD *nods.*

JOANNA. It sounds marvellous. You know, I think Donald's having you on, darling. He's really getting up his French so he and Les can have a naughty holiday together. (*Goes into the kitchen.*)

There is a silence, then the sound of saucepans from the kitchen. DONALD *sits.* LES *lifts his glass, sees it is empty and sets it down again.*

LES (*to* DONALD). I thought I'd ride up to Farlington.

DONALD. Oh. (*Nods.*)

LES. But I won't if you want to go up there next week.

DONALD. No, that's all right.

LES. Anyway, I can go and see what it's like, and we can go up again. Just take a quick look this time, you know, find out where the café is. (*Laughs.*)

DONALD *nods.*

LES (*pause*). Well, um, I suppose I'd better be getting on. (*Gets up.*)

HOWARTH. Yes – that's quite a trip, Farlington. (*Gets up.*)

DONALD. Yes. (*Also gets up.*)

JOANNA (*raises the hatch and speaks through it*). Darling, ask Les if he'll stay to lunch.

There is a pause.

HOWARTH. Les was just saying he was going to cycle up to Farlington.

JOANNA. Well, he'll be having lunch on the way, won't he? So why not have it here.

HOWARTH (*pause*). Yes, do.

LES. Well, I don't want to cause trouble.

HOWARTH. No trouble.

JOANNA. Well? Is he, or isn't he?

HOWARTH. Yes, he'd love to.

JOANNA. Good. (*Shuts hatch.*) Potatoes, darling!

HOWARTH *goes out.*

LES. How's it going, then?

DONALD. All right. (*Goes into his room, hangs up his coat on a chair.*)

LES (*looks at him, clearly worried and follows him to the doorway of the bedroom*). Is this your room then?

DONALD *comes out, sits down at the table and starts to get on with his work.*

I met your mum on the street – she was just coming back from church.

DONALD. Oh?

LES (*laughs*). She said to find out how they liked the cake.

DONALD. Oh. Yes, well, they liked it.

Pause.

LES (*sitting opposite* DONALD). Well, it's all right then, is it?

DONALD. What?

LES. Well, you know – everything.

DONALD *shrugs, looks at* LES.

(*Looks at him, looks down.*) Didn't you want me to stay to lunch, then?

DONALD *shrugs.*

I see. I'm sorry, Don. I mean, she asked me, didn't she. I didn't want to be rude to your friends. I didn't know *you* didn't want me.

DONALD (*after a pause, looking at* LES). Well, you know now, don't you. (*In a mutter.*)

LES *turns, goes out of the main door. The front door slams.* JOANNA *enters.*

JOANNA. Has Les gone?

DONALD (*gets up*). Um, Les had to go after all, he just remembered he had to do some shopping for his mum, and the shop'll be closed.

JOANNA. Oh!

DONALD. He said to say sorry.

Blackout

Scene Two

The Howarth living-room. Evening. The hatch is open, and through it come sounds of HOWARTH *and* DONALD *washing up, and their voices, quite distinct.* JOANNA *is at the piano, picking quietly the melody of 'Danny Boy'.*

HOWARTH. Maintenant, tu le prends *ou* vous le – ?

DONALD. Prenez . . .

HOWARTH. Pour le secher. Et moi, je vais laver cette assiette – donnez-le-moi, mon enfant, s'il vous plaît. Merci – oooops!

Sound of a plate crashing to the floor.
  JOANNA *stops playing the piano, looks towards the door.*

Well, what do you say now?

DONALD. Um, je suis desolé.

  HOWARTH *laughs.* JOANNA *cocks her head to one side, ironically.*

HOWARTH (*raising his voice*). Darling!

JOANNA (*slightly parodying*). Yes, darling?

HOWARTH (*looking in through hatch*). I'm afraid there's been a little – (*In French.*) – *accident*, darling.

JOANNA. Oh, that's all right, darling. Not to worry.

HOWARTH. It was only one of the plain white ones.

JOANNA. Oh, that's *good*.

HOWARTH. Sorry, darling.

  JOANNA *begins to play again.*

Non, non, laisse-la. Et le café, c'est prêt?

DONALD. Oui, c'est prêt.

HOWARTH. Bon – ça, c'est pour madame.

  DONALD, *wearing an apron, appears at the door, carrying a mug of coffee. He wipes the base of the mug on his apron and puts the coffee on the piano.*

JOANNA. Do you know the words?

DONALD. Well, um, not properly.

JOANNA. I bet you do.

DONALD. Well . . . (*Nods.*)

JOANNA. And sing them beautifully?

  DONALD *laughs, shakes his head.*

(*Smiles, and as* DONALD *turns to go.*) Come here.

DONALD *comes back apprehensively.*

(*Strikes a chord.*) Go on. Please.
DONALD. Well. (*Shakes his head, laughs.*) I can't.
JOANNA. Please! (*Plays again.*)

JOANNA *starts to sing the first few words.*

JOANNA. Oh, Danny Boy . . .

DONALD *joins in and they sing together.*

BOTH. . . . the pipes, the pipes are calling . . .

JOANNA *stops singing and* DONALD *goes on alone.*

DONALD. From glen to glen, and down the mountain side. The summer's gone and all the roses falling.

HOWARTH, *from the kitchen, puts a coffee mug on the hatch-shelf, moves quietly in to the doorway.*

'Tis you, 'tis you must go and I must bide.
But come ye back when summer's in the meadow
Or when the valley's . . .

HOWARTH *appears from the kitchen, wearing an apron and carrying a mug. He stays in the doorway, staring at* DONALD.

. . . hushed and white with snow,
And I'll be here, in sunshine or in shadow,
Oh Danny Boy, oh Danny Boy I love you so.
JOANNA (*ending the song*). I knew you'd have a beautiful voice.
HOWARTH. All the Irish do. It's because they're so sentimental.

HOWARTH *shuts the door.* DONALD *takes off the apron and leaves it on a chair.* HOWARTH *turns to the hatch, brings down the coffee mug there to* DONALD *at the table, puts his own coffee mug on the table.*

JOANNA *gets up, picks up her coffee cup and goes over to the sofa. She sits down and looks towards* DONALD. DONALD *sits at the table, gets his books and makes as if to begin some work.*

JOANNA. I'm sure you shouldn't, Donald. You've been at it all afternoon.

DONALD *looks at* HOWARTH.

HOWARTH (*looking up*). Perhaps you should give it a rest, but you can have a little dictation for a night cap, if you want.
JOANNA. So come and talk.

DONALD, *reluctantly, takes his coffee and sits by* JOANNA.

May we?
HOWARTH (*takes off his apron, sits at the table and begins marking books*). What? Mmm, go ahead.
JOANNA. He never minds when he's marking. Tell me more about your Paris adventure.
DONALD. Well, I'm, um, I don't think I'm going to Paris.

Glances towards HOWARTH.

JOANNA. Oh? (*Puzzled.*) Les seemed to think it was all arranged.
DONALD. Yes, well, I don't think I'll go. (*Clears his throat.*)
JOANNA. I'm sure you would have enjoyed it. I did at your age – and every age since. Won't Les be very disappointed?
DONALD (*shrugs*). Well, he can go on his own.
JOANNA. Will he? (HOWARTH *looks at them.*)
DONALD (*shrugs again, laughs awkwardly*). I don't know, but I'm not going.
JOANNA. I see. Wouldn't you enjoy Paris with Les, then?
DONALD (*shakes his head*). No.
JOANNA. Why not?
HOWARTH. Poor old Donald. He's getting quite a grilling.

JOANNA *looks towards him, shocked, then turns back to* DONALD. HOWARTH *looks back at his books.*

I'm sorry. (*Silkily.*) Am I grilling you?

DONALD. No. No, it's all right. (*Laughs.*)

JOANNA. I may ask you a question or two – by way of conversation?

> HOWARTH *lifts his head and looks towards them.* JOANNA *looks at* HOWARTH. DONALD *glances towards him.*

(*Very silkily.*) Well, may I, sir?

HOWARTH (*laughs*). Darling . . .

JOANNA. Good. (*Turning back to* DONALD.) You were saying you wouldn't enjoy Paris with Les.

DONALD. I just don't want to be with him – making his scenes and that.

JOANNA. Scenes? I thought you were friends.

DONALD. Not any more. He gets on my nerves.

JOANNA. I see. Poor Les, no wonder he didn't stay for lunch. (*Sips coffee.*)

HOWARTH. He didn't stay for lunch because he'd forgotten the shopping.

JOANNA (*looks at* HOWARTH, *pause, looks back at* DONALD). What does he do that gets on your nerves? (*Little pause. Looks at* HOWARTH.) May I ask? (*This meant genuinely.*)

DONALD (*glances at* HOWARTH). Well, he's odd. (JOANNA *looks back at* DONALD.) There's something wrong with him. He's always depending on me and nagging at me.

JOANNA. Well, I agree that does sound unpleasant – like a wife. (*Laughs. Looks at* HOWARTH.)

DONALD. Yes. (*Nervous laugh.*)

> JOANNA *looks back at* DONALD. *There is a pause as if the conversation is finished.* HOWARTH *goes back to his exercise book.*

JOANNA. Why do you think he's like that – with you?

> DONALD *looks across at* HOWARTH *for help.* JOANNA *follows his gaze across to* HOWARTH. HOWARTH *looks down at his books.*

Well, because, um, his feelings are confused. (*Little pause.*)
He's *a* homo- (*Checks himself.*) – sexual.

JOANNA (*after a pause*). Really? (*Pause.*) Has he told you he is?

> DONALD *glances towards* HOWARTH *again*. JOANNA *follows
> his glance*. HOWARTH *looks towards them, and pretends to go
> on correcting*.

DONALD. No, but I can see it now. I really knew it before. I
mean, from the way he was always depending on me and
making me apologize for things that were his fault. I always
knew there was something with him.

JOANNA. But what *exactly* put you onto him – it must have
been very recent. *He* certainly doesn't realize yet that you
know.

DONALD (*looks towards* HOWARTH. *There is a long, embarrassing
pause.* HOWARTH *looks at* DONALD). Well, um, Richard –
(JOANNA *turns to face* HOWARTH.) – when he saw him and
knew who he was from school, he warned me about him.

HOWARTH. I don't think I quite did that, Donald.

JOANNA. What *did* you say? (*Pleasantly.*) Or is it something
private that I oughtn't to know?

HOWARTH. Merely something to the effect that people are what
they are, and that we haven't the right to judge them. Donald
was slightly worried about Les's tendency to cling. He was
finding him a bit oppressive.

JOANNA. Clearly not the person to go to Paris with. (*To
DONALD.*)

DONALD. No, that's what Richard said too.

> JOANNA *looks at* HOWARTH.

HOWARTH. Well, again, not quite that, Donald. All I meant – or
at least meant to mean – was that if you're going to be forced
into someone's company a great deal, then you've got to be
sure of the company. I wasn't prescribing, I wouldn't dream
of doing so. (*Goes on with his marking.*)

JOANNA (*watches him*). But this thing at school – that you knew about. *Is* it private?

HOWARTH. No – well, yes, of course it is. (*Pause.*) It was just the usual schoolboy business. He got a crush on another boy, and there was a little – (*Shrugs.*) – trouble, but it's not for publication – I'm sure Donald knows that.

JOANNA. Well, I'll try and guard my tongue too. (*Ironically.*) But I suppose boys grow out of that. I actually wrote anonymous love letters to one of my teachers.

HOWARTH. The point is – (*Sharply.*) – that Donald – Les, I mean – hasn't grown out of it – at least from what Donald tells me. Anyway – (*Laughs.*) – it's a bit hard. He just dropped in to be, um, friendly, and we seem to be giving him a bit of a going-over between us. I mean what I said about not judging.

JOANNA. We are mean, aren't we? (*Looks at* HOWARTH, *clearly furious, gets up and goes out of the room into the kitchen and shuts the hatch from the other side.*)

There is a silence. HOWARTH *goes on marking.* DONALD *looks towards him, then looks down.*

HOWARTH (*marking, not looking up*). One of the facts of marriage, Donald, is that ladies, when in an advanced state of pregnancy, tend to be a trifle, um, dramatic, poor dears. Still – (*Looks at* DONALD.) – you will be careful never to repeat to anyone – and particularly Les – what I told you about him.

DONALD. Oh, no. (*Shakes his head.*) No.

HOWARTH. Anyway, perhaps you'd better get an early night, eh? – in view of tomorrow. (*Turns, smiles at him.*)

DONALD (*rising*). I thought we were going to do that last dictation, you said. I'll be all right for that.

HOWARTH (*hesitates, then regretfully*). I think we've left it a bit late really.

DONALD. Oh. (*Disappointed.*)

HOWARTH. Goodnight.

DONALD (*takes the dictionary and satchel, makes for his bedroom door – stops, turns, looks at* HOWARTH). If – if I get through my 'O' level, would you help me then? With my 'A' levels?

HOWARTH. I don't know, Donald.

> DONALD *looks at him for a moment, then turns, goes into the bedroom. He turns on the light there, puts down the satchel, takes off his tie, hesitates, picks up the dictionary and returns to the living-room.*

DONALD. I just remembered – I mean, I might forget it in the morning. *(Puts it down on the table.)*

HOWARTH. Oh yes, I can't let you have all the luck, can I? Someone else may need it sometime. *(Smiles.)* I've got a lot going on at school at the moment, and next term – when I've finished with that blasted Bishop – I've got to organize the French play, and then I've got the football, the colts, and of course there'll be the baby. *(Smiles.)* But I'm sure we'll manage *something* – for your 'A' levels.

DONALD. Thank you, Richard.

HOWARTH. Because, you know, you're going to pass tomorrow – and I want you to go on. I intend to take all the credit.

> DONALD *smiles.*

Now you go to bed.

> DONALD *turns, goes back to the room.* HOWARTH *goes back to his marking.*
> *There is a pause. The door opens.* JOANNA *comes in, picks up the cups, etc., then goes out again.* HOWARTH *watches her. She comes in again.*

JOANNA. Donald gone to bed?

HOWARTH. Yes. What about you?

JOANNA. Has he gone to the bathroom yet?

HOWARTH. Um, I don't know. I don't think so.

> JOANNA *sits down.*

You going?

JOANNA. In a minute. (*Coldly*.)

> HOWARTH *looks at her, then turns back to his marking.* DONALD *comes out of the room, in trousers and shirt with sponge bag. He looks towards* JOANNA *and* HOWARTH, *then hurries out.*

Now then, what the hell were you up to?

HOWARTH. What do you mean?

JOANNA. Were you trying to put me in my place?

HOWARTH (*laughs contemptuously*). Of course not.

JOANNA. Then I assume your odd turns of phrase – grilling, going over, etc. – were an attempt to cover up your own indiscretions.

HOWARTH. What indiscretions?

JOANNA. Your revelations about Les – but then you were covering a lot of territory – moral and psychological – do you do that with all your boys?

HOWARTH. You're being very offensive. (*Little pause, they stare at each other*.) The occasion doesn't usually arise. He asked me my advice about Les and I gave it to him. Yes, come to think of it, I'd do that with any boy – I consider it part of my job. He simply got hold of the wrong end of the stick, that's all.

JOANNA. Well, that's certainly a bad omen for his examination – if he makes such a hash of understanding you in English.

> HOWARTH *shrugs.*

Well?

HOWARTH. Well? (*Little pause, he throws his pen down on the table*.) What do you want me to do – tell him he's a bloody little fool for getting it wrong? I've already been extremely tactless with him once today, the last thing I want to do is mess him up again, especially with the examination in the morning. With the chance he's got.

JOANNA. Richard. (*Pause*.) Richard, look at me, please. (*Politely*.)

HOWARTH. What?

JOANNA. That's better. You've been dodging your eyes all round me for weeks – except once or twice when you've glared at me. (*Looks away.*) Perhaps I'm not very pleasant to look at.

HOWARTH. What?

JOANNA. Do you think I don't know? Nine months of just getting fatter and squatter, and going on at you about foetal stages and membranes splitting and shows of water and bottles of urine, not to mention vomiting at the beginning and lying all over the place now. Do you think *I* don't feel it – with *my* tendency to cling?

HOWARTH. Don't be silly.

JOANNA. And off and on I think, who *would* want to lie beside this swollen sow, *not* flower, and then I think, well, hell, it's just as much your doing, so you can damn well lie beside me and like it. (*She smiles sadly.*) But you don't like it, you haven't liked it for months, and there's nothing I can do about that. Nothing at all. I can't stop you from being disgusted by me, not by law or love.

HOWARTH. Disgusted?

JOANNA. Don't do that. Not now. If you need time to think, just ask for an intermission. I won't scream.

> HOWARTH *gets up, goes over to her, bends down, kisses her on the cheek and sits beside her.*

Thank you. But think about it. When did you last kiss me properly? When I was three months gone?

> *The door opens,* DONALD *comes in.*

DONALD (*turning, smiling*). 'Night, Joanna.

JOANNA. 'Night, Donald.

DONALD. 'Night, Richard.

HOWARTH. Donald.

> DONALD *goes on into his room, puts down his sponge bag and clothes, turns out the light and gets into bed. There is a pause.* HOWARTH *attempts to kiss her properly.*

JOANNA. Don't be ridiculous. (*Gently.*) Do you know what I've found out this weekend? I don't like good teachers.

HOWARTH. Don't you?

JOANNA. They really are self-indulgent. All this business with Donald – moralising, philosophising, gossiping, weeping, advising – it's just self-indulgence. You don't know anything about anything at all, not really.

HOWARTH (*smiling*). Not really.

JOANNA. Least of all yourself.

HOWARTH. Least of all myself.

JOANNA. And you're not, actually, charming me one little bit. (*Gets up.*)

HOWARTH (*gets up*). Darling . . .

JOANNA. This isn't a good time to find you out.

> HOWARTH *steps back, as if he's been hit.* JOANNA *turns, goes to the door.*

HOWARTH. You can't leave it just like that –

JOANNA. You're busy.

HOWARTH. That can wait, darling! I – (*Gestures to the exercise books.*)

JOANNA. No, it can't wait. You be as long as you like, Richard. Because I'm bloody tired and want to be asleep. (*Opens the door, goes out, closes the door.*)

> HOWARTH *stands for a moment, makes a gesture of frustration and anger, then goes to the door, stands there, hesitating, then opens the door and goes into the hall as if to call* JOANNA. *Pause. He goes into the kitchen and comes back munching on a biscuit, looks at* DONALD's *door, then sits down, carrying the biscuit tin and begins marking. There is a slight dimming of light in the lounge to suggest the passing of time.*

DONALD (*as the lights start to fade, cries out in his sleep*). Please . . . please . . . please . . .!

> *The lights fade out and fade up again. In the living-room the*

centre table-lamp on the shelves is on, with just a pool of light round the table where HOWARTH *is still working. In the bedroom, the lights are on and* DONALD *is discovered, moaning and rocking himself to and fro on the chair, still asleep.* HOWARTH *hears the sounds, rises and goes to the bedroom door, knocks. No answer.*

HOWARTH. Donald, Donald – (*He goes in, leaves the door open.*) Donald! Donald!

He gently puts his hand on DONALD's *shoulder.* DONALD *wakes with a start, looks up at* HOWARTH.

It's all right, Donald. It's all right.

DONALD. I'm sorry, Richard, I'm sorry.

DONALD *suddenly clasps* HOWARTH *round the waist, burying his face against him.* HOWARTH *gently raises* DONALD *up from the chair.* DONALD *puts his arms round* HOWARTH.

HOWARTH. There's nothing for you to be frightened of. Not here.

DONALD *starts to cry.*

Donald, don't. Don't. (*Puts his arms round him.*) There there, my Donald, there, my dear old Donald. There, I'm on your side. I care about you, you know I care about you. I'll see that nothing can harm you.

Still embracing DONALD, *but now with more feeling, he closes the door, then takes* DONALD's *head in both his hands and turns his face to his.*
The lights fade out.

(*As the lights are fading.*) Donald, Donald . . .

After a pause a beam of light comes up in the living-room, focused on the back of the sofa. JOANNA, *in dressing-gown, is*

seated there, her head bowed. She raises her head to face the
bedroom door and a beam of light comes up in the bedroom,
focused on the chair beside the door. HOWARTH *is sitting*
there, head raised. DONALD *is in bed, but the bed and the rest*
of the bedroom is in darkness. HOWARTH *looks at* DONALD,
gets up slowly and leaves the bedroom for the living-room,
closing the door. The light fades in the bedroom and increases
in the living-room.

HOWARTH *steps into the living-room and is going towards the*
door when he sees JOANNA. *They stay staring at each other*
for a long time, then JOANNA *rises and slowly goes to the door*
and opens it. HOWARTH *slowly goes past her and out of the*
room. JOANNA *follows and closes the door.*

After a pause the morning light slowly builds, strong sunlight
seen through the curtains which are still shut, and we are into
Scene Three.

Scene Three

The Howarth living-room. Morning.

DONALD *wakes, sits up in bed, hunched over for a minute. He hears a*
noise from the kitchen and gets quickly out of bed and starts desper-
ately and hurriedly to dress, takes off his pyjama jacket and puts on
his shirt, does not stop to put on his tie.

JOANNA *enters, looks towards the bedroom door, crosses to the*
window and opens the curtains by their pulley cord. Morning light
floods the room. She crosses to the table, pushes the school books
downstage on the table to make way for the tray, slowly goes out
again to the kitchen. After a pause she returns with a tray having
on it tea, bread and butter and knives and forks, places it on the up-
stage side of the table. All this while DONALD *has been hurriedly*
dressing and cramming his possessions into the carrier bag. JOANNA
leaves the table and has reached the door when DONALD, *dressed and*

carrying his bag and satchel starts to open the door. He sees JOANNA *and leaps back into the bedroom, begins to close the door.*

JOANNA (*still in her dressing-gown, sees the door closing*). Donald!

DONALD (*opens the door slowly, carrying the carrier bag and satchel*). Um, 'morning, Joanna.

JOANNA. Good morning, Donald. Your breakfast's ready. Would you sit down?

> DONALD *sits at the table.* JOANNA *goes out into the kitchen.* DONALD *puts his things on the floor beside him.* JOANNA *returns with a plate of scrambled egg.*

Here you are. (*Sets the plate down in front of him on the tray and starts to pour him out a cup of tea.*) What time have you got to get to work?

DONALD. I'm going to the examination hall. It's in the town hall. Um, at nine o'clock.

JOANNA. Well, you'd better hurry then, it's already half-past eight. Sugar? (*Passes him the basin from the other side of the tray.*)

> DONALD *nods, helps himself to sugar.* JOANNA *sits by the table, watching him.* DONALD *drinks tea, his hand trembling and slowly starts to eat the egg, acutely conscious of her presence.* JOANNA *rises slowly, takes the biscuit tin from the table up to the hatch, puts it through and closes the hatch. She continues watching* DONALD. DONALD *takes another sip of tea and one more forkful of egg to his lips. He can't eat, looks at* JOANNA, *puts the fork down.*

All right? Nothing else I can give you?

DONALD. No, thank you. No. That was very nice. Um – (*Gets up and picks up his things.*)

JOANNA (*goes over to the door*). Richard! Donald's just leaving. (*Goes out to the kitchen.*)

DONALD *stares nervously towards the door, his arms full with bag and satchel.*

HOWARTH (*enters*). Good morning, Donald. Condemned man ate a hearty, um – (*Gestures towards the table – there is an appalling silence.*) My God, your dictionary. (*Goes to the table, picks it up, hands it to* DONALD.)

DONALD. Um, no, it's yours. (*Tries to hand it back.*)

HOWARTH. I know, but – look. I want you to have it, it's a very lucky dictionary, I –

DONALD. I – I – can't. (*Shakes his head, tries to give it back.*)

HOWARTH. Why not?

DONALD. Well, it's not – I mean, it's too er . . .

HOWARTH. Nonsense, bloody nonsense, it's not too anything, except wrong of you not to let me give it to you. I – I need you to have it, Donald. Please.

DONALD (*takes the dictionary emotionally*). Thank you, Richard. (*Looks down at it.*) You won't be helping me with my 'A' levels, then?

HOWARTH (*gently*). No, Donald.

DONALD *nods, suddenly makes a low, sobbing noise.*

DONALD. I don't know what I'm going to do. (*He starts to cry.*)

HOWARTH (*shuts the door quickly and goes back towards* DONALD, *not close to him*). Donald – what, look, what happened, it was one of those, well, the kind of thing, it could happen to anybody, it caught us, um, me, the thing is to forget what happened, in the end it won't matter, but try to remember me as a teacher. And a friend. I am your friend, Donald.

DONALD. Yes, Richard.

HOWARTH. It won't matter, nothing will matter except that we, we liked each other, from our different, um, rafts. (*Long pause, puts his hand on* DONALD'S *shoulder, glances towards the door.*) And when you've got your 'O' levels and all the 'A' levels you want, because you will, Donald, and when you're doing, doing – (*Moving away.*) – what you want to do, think of that, eh?

DONALD. Sir.

HOWARTH. And Donald – if – well, you won't tell anyone about it, will you, ever? Not Les – no one?

DONALD (*looks down, whispers*). No, sir.

DONALD. I'm sorry, sir. I'm very sorry.

Pause.

JOANNA *comes in.*

JOANNA (*entering to between them*). It's getting on.

HOWARTH. Yes, you'd better go.

JOANNA *sees the dictionary* DONALD *is holding.*

JOANNA (*tentatively*). Isn't that ours? (*Looks at* HOWARTH.)

DONALD (*holding out the book as if to offer it back*). Well – Richard said –

JOANNA. Oh, I see.

She goes to DONALD *and gently pushes the book back into his hands.*

Good luck in your examination, Donald.

DONALD. Thank you, Joanna.

HOWARTH (*still at other side of sofa*). Yes, Donald, good luck.

DONALD. Thank you, sir.

JOANNA goes out. DONALD *follows without looking back. Pause.* HOWARTH *slowly crosses to a chair by the table, pulls it away from the table and sits. Pause.* JOANNA *returns, closes the door. She is carrying the cake-box. She crosses down to* HOWARTH, *to his left and holds the box out to him.*

JOANNA. To say thank you with.

CURTAIN